Boogie Time

Boogie Time

Vernon S. C. Castle

Dynasty
Press

Boogie Time

Dynasty Press Limited
36 Ravensdon Street
London SE11 4AR

First published by Dynasty Press Ltd.

ISBN : 978-1-5272-0445-4
eBook ISBN: 978-1-911350-15-6

Cover artwork design by **Rupert Dixon & Vernon Castle**

Book Design by **Biddles Books**

Table of Contents

To all our teachers,
upon whose shoulders we stand, reaching for our dreams.

July 17th

I
Northeastern Pacific
Aboard the 45' sloop *Dickies Treat*

Earl Levin was in his late sixties, but casual observers could be forgiven for thinking him ten years younger. At the wheel, his thick, silver grey hair rippled in the breeze. His deeply tanned face held aquamarine eyes that were cool and confident, maybe a bit cruel. He noticed with some annoyance the backs of his wrinkled hands on the wheel, the age spots grown larger and denser in the last few years.

"Life at sea, rough on the hands," he would joke when someone noticed and commented. Except the sea Earl mostly sailed flowed in and around Wall Street as he captained Newbury Corp through the shoals and tempests of the financial world.

Earl had retired last year though and was indeed the captain of a new ship. His lifelong hobby of "sailing when he could" had taken a serious turn when he purchased *Dickies Treat* in Naples. He'd spent the last summer in the Mediterranean getting to know her. With the help of onboard automation he could handle her alone but preferred to have company on board. Especially if the company was female and fun in the sack.

A clatter of plates from the galley drew his attention below, just in time to see Véronique ascending the stairs. She held a tray with a couple of champagne flutes. Also, he noted approvingly, some of the caviar snacks she made so well. In her other hand she gripped a bottle of Moët & Chandon on the neck, swinging it casually by her side. Not for the first time, Earl was struck by the dangerous beauty she exuded. Ready for a good time or ready for trouble. You pick it. It was one of the attractions when he met her at the Royal Yacht Club in Hong Kong.

Earl had had more than a few crewmates with benefits since he left the Mediterranean via Suez. Lots of comings and goings, making his way along India and through Southeast Asia. But Véronique was the pick of the litter. Almost as tall as himself, at six foot one, with dark, almond shaped eyes that sparkled mischievously when she called him "her pirate". At thirty-six she seemed at the peak of her sexual power. Earl liked the way eyes followed them when they moved through a room together. She wore her long blond hair in plaits down her back, framing her perfect oval face with shoulder length wisps that accented her refined cheekbones. She knew how to sensually reveal her athletic figure. Her long legs were perfectly suited to the Hong Kong style split dresses she wore.

Earl knew she was bright and determined. He'd seen the type coming up the corporate ladder for years. They thought they were playing him, but it was the other way around. It was a no-brainer to offer her a berth on the reach over to Seattle from Hong Kong.

"Seattle," she had cooed. "How perfect that you are going to that place, it is the home of my brother and sister. I'm tired of Asia. You shall take me there." It was a pronouncement Earl could see no reason to argue with. Later that night, she gave him every reason to keep his bargain.

As she stepped out of the galley and placed the tray on the little side table, Earl let himself enjoy her exquisite backside, the expanse of bare back and the little yellow bikini bottoms. The cork popped and she poured, turning to offer Earl a glass. Her bare breasts were firm, almost conical. The dark nipples had a charming upturn. Véronique watched Earl's eyes move up from her breasts to meet her gaze. It amused her, the power she had over this man.

"Chin chin," she smiled. They tapped glasses and sipped, keeping their eyes on each other.

The reach across the Northern Pacific can be as treacherous as any in the world, but at this time of year it was relatively smooth sailing. Earl felt very confident in his skills as a sailor, and had satisfied himself in these last months that he was up to the challenge. His satellite connection assured that no big weather would catch them by surprise. The route necessarily took him through the zone called the Pacific Gyre, a slowly rotating gigantic eddy bigger than Texas. The gyre had the unfortunate reputation of being a repository of current borne refuse, particularly plastics. Earl had seen firsthand the almost omnipresent deluge of plastic garbage in his voyages, there were virtually no beaches in the Mediterranean that were not littered with bits of styrofoam and plastic bottles. It was much the same through the Indian Ocean and the waters around Indonesia and the Philippines.

Earl tried to take it in stride. After all, his Newbury Corp dealt in the international plastics trade and the profits from that trade had seen him handsomely rewarded. *Dickies Treat* was his because of plastics. In the big picture, the world is a better place because of plastics. The sterile IV bags from Newbury had saved countless lives, as had their entire line of single use medical supplies. Infection rates were down all across the board. Of course the waste stream was significant, but not all that difficult to deal with. Hell, in most small communities in Denmark high efficiency incinerators turned the waste stream into nonpolluting electrical power for local consumption. We could do the same thing in the States except for all the mindless jerks who said, "Not in my backyard."

"Caviar?" Véronique held the tray out to Earl, and he selected one of the halved croissants. The rich crème fraiche with a hint of horseradish topped with beluga caviar went perfectly with the champagne.

"Thanks Sugar. Nobody does it better."

"You are welcome. I'm going forward to read and take some sun, OK?" Véronique smiled.

"Umm," replied Earl.

His gaze followed her shapely rear as it swayed down the top deck to the little gazebo forward. Véronique settled on a chaise. Beyond her, Earl noticed a dark smudge on the eastern horizon. What the hell was that? It reminded him of coming into LA by air, the curtain of smog brooding over the city. This couldn't be smog way out here. Or could it? Probably the goddamned Chinese smog blowing east. Earl checked his heading and they were dead on for Seattle. "Just have to plow through it," he thought. It was incredible how the Chinese could make as much air pollution as they wanted and just have it blow over to the USA.

The wind was with him and, while steady, it wasn't too brisk. The GPS indicated they'd come about forty-six miles since breakfast five hours ago. Earl quickly calculated on the autopilot control screen. "Well, we're making about eight knots. That's not too bad," he thought. He poured another glass of champagne and helped himself to a caviar snack. "Time to catch up on some correspondence," he reflected ruefully, "You can be done with New York but it's never done with you, even in retirement."

Flipping on the full autopilot function he dropped down into the galley and opened his laptop. Harold, the new CEO of Newbury, was annoyingly insistent about getting Earl's thoughts on the Canadian expansion. He gazed for a moment at the screensaver photo, a nice shot of Adam and Lucy from

Christmas five years back. You'd think they'd have got over his divorce by now. Adam was, what, thirty three, Lucy thirty one. They weren't kids anymore, but Maryanne had blamed him for everything and the kids had taken her side. You'd think they'd know better.

Earl's attention shifted to the sound of the sea on the hull. It had changed to a gentle, sibilant whisper, as if the water outside was mirror flat. He didn't really feel like writing to Harold so he snapped the laptop shut and went back up on deck. He peered over the starboard rail. What was that?

The sea was indeed calm, but the surface was almost completely covered by a black velvet mat. Oil spill? He hadn't heard of anything. Over the edge, along the hull, *Dickies Treat* had a bathtub ring of some king of black ooze.

"Shit. That will be a nice clean-up job."

Earl grabbed a line hook pole and leaned over to get a light scraping of the stuff adhering to the hull. "Hmm," he rubbed it between his fingers. "Not oil. More of a scum, like an algae." It rinsed off easily enough from the pole and his hand. "Black algae?" he wondered.

He sat back on the rear bench, running a moist hand across his forehead. "Champagne in the afternoon," he mused, "Going right to my head." He felt genuinely woozy sitting there in the warm afternoon, even with the cool breeze.

Baap! Baap! Baap!

The alarm in the galley was sounding.

"What the hell? Did she leave the stove on or something?" Earl headed down the gangway steps and almost lost his footing. He was really feeling the champagne.

Baap! Baap! Baap!

It wasn't the fire alarm he realized with some relief. A quick look around revealed no smoke. The stove was off.

Baap! Baap! Baap!

The little round alarm over the engine compartment door was the culprit. The carbon monoxide alarm. How could that be? The engine wasn't even running. Was it? Earl opened the door down to the little engine room and flipped on the light. Everything shipshape here.

Baap! Baap! Baap!

He pressed the defeat button on the alarm housing to stop the infernal wailing and gave the whole unit a twist, removing it from the wall. Battery? Opening the little housing, he removed the nine volt battery and touched the contacts to his tongue. The sudden bitter tingle said the battery was fine, plenty of juice.

"What is going on?"

Earl turned back into the galley and the alarm slipped from his hands and fell to the floor. It seemed to fall in slow motion. A sudden bout of dizziness caused him to grab the door frame to steady himself.

A heavy thud topside and a splash.

Earl struggled out into the cockpit and saw, over the starboard rail, a prone body slipping past in the water. Face down, long blond hair fouled with the algae, skimpy yellow bottoms polka-dotted with the stuff.

Earl slumped down, hanging over the rail, watching Véronique fall behind.

"A little slower now. Must be doing less than eight knots."

That was the last thought Earl had before darkness swallowed his mind.

II
Mountain View, California
NOAA Global Atmospheric Survey Monitor Station

Dan Holmes popped another Cheeto into his mouth and crunched down. The new crunchy Cheetos were better than the big old soft orange wads from when he was a kid.

"Hey Nancy!" he called.

Nancy looked up from her bank of monitors, more harassed than interested.

"What Dan. What now?"

He smiled. "It looks like NOAA is going to get eighty percent funding now."

She thought the orange Cheeto scum across his teeth very unattractive. "And where did you get that fine piece of news, Mr. Holmes?" she asked.

Dan tapped one of the monitors at his station. "Good old CSPAN. Just posted the vote in Congress. Looks like we both keep our jobs."

The Global Atmosphere Survey monitoring station wasn't on the block. NOAA needed the data on greenhouse gas levels that the GAS satellite network provided. What was on the block was the human component. Some of the higher-ups argued that a full time human staff was redundant. AI was sufficiently capable of filtering the data and disseminating it to analysts.

"Then maybe," Nancy suggested, "you should turn off CSPAN and start doing the job they're funding you for." She leaned in closer to one of her monitors, brow furrowed. "For example, bring up GAS 017 and tell me what you see."

Dan tapped at his keyboard and one of his monitors flickered and changed view. He studied the image for a moment. "On 017? I see nice weather in the Northwest Pacific."

"Go to IR."

Dan hit a key and the infrared image appeared. "Hm. Well, there's a warm cell about six hundred miles out. A big one, huh?" He tapped a few other keys. "It's about one point two Celsius above the general. A high pressure maybe?"

"No, I don't think so. Barometrics don't conform. Let's try something else." She configured for methane. Some models predicted oceanic methane burps with the warming. They were already seeing serious outgassing up in Siberia as the permafrost reduced. Some big releases of methane hydrate off the Arctic coast too, but nothing this big.

"Hmm." Dan had come over to her station and his Cheeto breath was annoying. "Doesn't look like a methane signal. You know, that is pretty much centered over the gyre, a little shift to the east. Maybe all that garbage is rotting," he grinned.

Nancy shrugged. "If it was the usual landfill type decomposition, you'd see the gas signature here," she tapped the satellite image. "Let's try carbon dioxide." The image shifted to the light green of carbon dioxide, but the target area was no different than the surrounding zone, reading out at point zero three seven two. "Nope. Dead end there," she said.

Dan leaned in, invading her space. "I'm betting it's just a dead zone right now. No wind and it's heating up. Wouldn't want to be out there in a sailboat right now. Becalmed."

She had leaned away from his intrusion and now he seated himself on the chair beside her, backwards, resting his arms on the backrest. "Now with the right company, becalmed could be a very good thing, don't you think?"

Nancy brushed a handful of her auburn hair behind an ear and met his gaze. "Dan," she smiled sweetly, "go fuck yourself."

He laughed and stood. "Well, we're losing 017. Let's get 013 programed to do a total comp reading when it comes over in," he looked at his watch, "one hour and twenty minutes."

"I'll be gone, but you and Ed can have fun with that one," Nancy responded.

Dan returned to his station and called back, "This is why an AI will never replace me." He hunched over his keyboard and began the sequence for the 013 survey program.

Nancy wondered if it would take an AI three years to figure out she wasn't interested.

III
Northeastern Pacific
Aboard the Maersk container ship, *Kentang Goring*

Charlie Baskin was jolted awake by the sharp metallic crash near his head. He felt the mask on his face and reflexively tried to brush it away. Then memory flooded back into his confused consciousness.

"What the hell? Where am I?"

More gently now he touched the mask, feeling the bag below his chin inflate as he inhaled. The white walls of the infirmary and the big red cross on the glass window in the door. He took another breath.

"Oh shit." Tentatively, he felt the top of his head, the rough stubble from the burn. His forehead too, all the bubbled blisters. Being startled awake he had tried to sit up, but the screaming pain in his scalded skin had been instantly sobering. He rested back in bed as full consciousness returned.

There had been a fire alarm in cargo forward. Kim, Greg and he had suited up and rushed down to help a dozen others who were already dragging out the hose. A withering heat and orange white flames rocketed up and out towards them. No way to see if it was cargo or a fuel line rupture. He remembered holding the nozzle with Kim, the force of the water threatening to knock them off their feet. There was that moment when one of the guys struck the bulkhead door with a fire axe. At that instant he wanted to shout "No!" Then came the explosion. The fireball engulfed him, the screaming pain, white hot demons tearing the flesh off his bones, Kim's face a shriek of burned back lips. Then here.

Consciousness had surfaced a few times. The morphine made the memory floaty. Charlie took another breath. He had eyes. His feet, he could feel his feet under the sheets. Both hands, both arms. Everything felt there. The burns were from the chest up. What did he look like? Eyelids? He could feel teeth and tongue and lips. Maybe not too bad.

Charlie lay there, waiting for the medic to come in. Dr. Lawlor. That's right. He was a nice old guy. Where was he?

He needed to piss. When was somebody going to come in?

"Hello?" he tried to call through the mask. He was still on the oxygen. The memory of Dr. Lawlor: "Son, you were just plain lucky. That chlorine did a job on your lungs though. Gonna be some time in healing. You just rest now."

Chlorine? Where had that come from? Where was everybody? Where were Kim and Greg? Charlie lifted slightly and looked over the left side of the bed. On the floor two metal trays and a scattering of implements. And somebody. He couldn't see who. Black shoes and dark trousers, white lab coat, dark hair, hands sprawled out in front.

He knew the large green tank standing beside the bed was oxygen. The regulator had a flex tube leading to the bag of his mask. Slightly cool oxygen flowed in from the bottom. When he exhaled, he heard the little exhaust valves flex and then re-seat. It reminded him of clearing his snorkel when he went diving in the Philippines. That had been a good trip. His sweetheart, Duck, had been such a good sport. She was so petite and yet such a fighter! The slums of Manilla either kill you or make you invincible.

Why doesn't somebody come?

"Hello!" Charlie croaked again.

Nothing.

He glanced up at the oxygen tank. The regulator had a pressure gauge that read "Fifteen". Fifteen what? His body was going to piss. Charlie clenched his teeth and slowly sat upright, swinging his feet out from under the covers and down onto the cool floor. It hurt, but he slowly rolled out of the bed into a hunched standing position. His hands were bandaged up to the forearms, but he could steady himself against the wall. He knew there was a head around the corner. The tube from his mask wouldn't reach so he clumsily and painfully removed the headpiece and worked his way along the wall. He had to step over the man on the floor, as he did so he bent to examine him. It was Bentley. Dead as a doornail, but flushed red, even cherry red, lips. Cherry red lips!

Charlie felt a chill even through the ache of the burn. He knew first aid. They all did, it was required. Cherry red lips meant carbon monoxide poisoning, the kind of thing you see when somebody decided to check out by closing the garage door and leaving the motor running. Morticians loved it. Bentley's corpse looked all rosy and fresh. No muss, no fuss.

Had the fire made a bunch of CO? How could it be here? This was later. The fire had to be out. How long have I been here?

Charlie straightened up and made it into the head to pee. He knew the lightheadedness he was beginning to feel meant oxygen deprivation. As quickly as he could he returned to the bed and held the mask in place, breathing regularly until his head started to clear. Was it just this room? He took a deep breath and hobbled to the infirmary door. Looking down the hall, he got his answer. Twenty feet ahead another crewman lay sprawled on the floor.

Retreating back to the mask, Charlie secured it in place. The ship telephone on the wall was within reach. He felt relief to hear the dial tone and punched up 001, The Bridge. It rang. No answer after twenty tones. 002, First Mate. No answer. In his guts, he knew nobody was going to answer and replaced the phone in its wall cradle.

"Dying of thirst here," he thought and opened the little refrigerator under the work bench. A nearly full bottle of apple juice. Charlie took a deep breath, lifted the mask and drank most of the juice in one go.

"Got to get up to the bridge somehow. Find help."

The answer. Two levels below the infirmary was the tool shop. And the diving gear. If the ship was somehow flooded with carbon monoxide, the scuba tank would give him an hour of air. He had to try.

He sat on the bed for a time, feeling his weakness and resenting it. Charlie was grateful for the mask, grateful that it was the non-rebreather type. No mixing with the room air. He could hear the voice of Mrs. James, his first aid instructor: "Carbon monoxide wants your red blood cells a hundred times more than oxygen does. Do you see what that means? If a room had plenty of oxygen and only one part in a hundred of carbon monoxide, you'd die of suffocation. Oxygen can't compete with CO when it comes to your blood."

She had gone on to describe some of the dumb things people had done, accidentally killing themselves. Like using charcoal briquettes inside a van to keep warm on a skiing trip. "They thought they'd be OK since there was no open flame." And that family at the Marina in San Francisco who'd let their boat idle to keep the generator going while they slept. Found them all dead in their bunks below come morning.

If the whole boat had filled with carbon monoxide from the fire, he might be the only one left alive. After five more minutes on the pure oxygen, he took a last, long deep breath and turned off the tank valve. Best save what he could.

Charlie caught his face in the mirror on the way to the

infirmary door and gasped. The hair would probably grow back, but there was going to be some serious facial scarring. What the hell. He was alive. Painfully and slower than he would have liked, he made his way down the interior stairwell to the workshop and diving gear. First order of business was to mount a regulator and start breathing. He'd come across three more crewmates along the way, including Swank, the Chief, draped over his desk in the workshop area.

There were six tanks, each holding about seventy-two cubic feet of air, if they were full. He hoped they were.

Once he started the flow of air and slipped on the backpack with the tank, he fashioned wet tissue into nose plugs and blocked off his nasal passages. Didn't want to do any accidental breathing down here. It was a pain in the ass to do all this with bandaged hands, but it worked.

So far, the electricity was on and the engines of the big ship sounded steady. This can't have happened very long ago. To his relief, the service elevator door slid open as always and he punched up the bridge level. When the door opened, the crumpled form of Whit Carson lay in the corner. Whit was getting married when they got back to Seattle. But not now.

He stepped onto the bridge. Everything appeared normal, radar operational, all A-OK. Except the Captain and First Mate lay dead on the floor, and Romney, the little capuchin monkey, hung limply from his chain, eyes bugged out, swinging gently.

Charlie moved down the bridge and out into the fresh air. Outside, the sun was bright, the sky clear. Thank God. It may be poisonous within the confines of the ship, but out here in the breeze, under the open sky he could breathe freely, think about what to do. The autopilot was engaged, the course into the harbor at Seattle set, as best as he could see. They'd have to send a pilot out, of course, but he needed to alert the Coast Guard, now.

"Should I call the home office?" he wondered. "What's with the smog?"

Charlie stood in the breeze and began to notice the surface of the sea that the *Kentang* steamed across. It was blanketed with some sort of black velvet, a Sargasso Sea or something. Then he noticed several things simultaneously: He was beginning to feel the light headedness of oxygen deprivation. The bridge walkway and lower decks had a number of dead seagulls and a large dead pelican. The usual escort of sea birds that followed was nowhere in sight. The air itself was poison!

Charlie replaced the tank mouthpiece and began breathing deeply, trying to flush his system. He fumbled for the door handle, feeling sluggish and muddled. Fear gripped him that he had inhaled enough CO that the fresh air of the tank had come too late. For the next fifteen minutes he stood on the bridge hyperventilating, weak, forcing himself to remain conscious. If he passed out here he was done for. Too depleted to make it back to the pure oxygen of the infirmary. He hoped and prayed and clung to life.

Slowly, his head began to clear. The gauge on his regulator said he had five hundred pounds of pressure remaining. At sea level, maybe twenty more minutes of air. He had to get a Mayday out, had to let somebody know.

Dialing out on the radio maritime emergency band, Charlie almost burst into tears when a voice at the other end answered, "Coast Guard Emergency."

IV
Mountain View, California
NOAA Global Atmospheric Survey Monitor Station

Dan exhaled slowly, looking at the monitor. Ed stood behind him and spoke.

"Carbon monoxide? How could there be a vast cell of almost two percent CO in the middle of the Pacific Ocean?"

"It's not quite in the middle," Dan replied. "It's more over the eastern part of the Pacific Gyre, closer to the coast."

"Well it seems to be staying contained there. Monitor says it's dissipating as it blows east. Whatever the causal agent, it looks to be localized."

"Yeah," Dan agreed, "but if that mass moved east, we'd be looking at a complete evacuation from the middle of BC to Northern California."

"Time to make some phone calls," Ed said.

Dan nodded.

"Yup."

July 18th

Oakland, California
Citigen Corporation

"Legumes do it," Kyle smiled. "It's not unnatural."

"It's unnatural to cut into what God has given us, to play God. You don't have that right. You don't have the wisdom!"

Joan Riser bristled. The smug self-assurance of the young man was infuriating.

Kyle often spent a few minutes talking with the protestors at the gates of Citigen, a daily gauntlet he had to run on his way into the lab. He defended the practice to some of his colleagues. "Come on, we all know that civil discourse and education are key factors here. There's so much fear and misinformation out there. We owe it to them and to ourselves. Personally, if I can't explain and defend my research rationally then maybe I shouldn't be doing it. Am I right?"

Dave Davenport sighed. Kyle was a good man - bright, idealistic, the future of the company. But he also knew that trying to be rational with the irrational was like trying to cajole a mad dog out of rabies. "Kyle, you know I am wholeheartedly in agreement with your motivations. You're right. Absolutely. People are afraid of what they don't understand. Hell, sometimes they're afraid even when they do understand. I know that as a person. We all know it as a company."

Dave liked to think of Citigen as a sort of Camelot, a place of promise and intelligence and magic. In the uproar of anti-GMO and pro-GMO forces, Citigen had quietly and competently been making strides in reducing pesticide and fertilizer use, creating the tools for agriculture to succeed on marginal, arid and saline lands. It wasn't flash and didn't get much press exposure, and maybe that was a good thing. As his old man used to say, the high nail gets the hammer. Certain interests had successfully painted Monsanto as Satan and now wanted to tar others with the same brush. He knew that neither he nor Kyle nor anybody else was going to alter the new religion and its true believers.

"Sometimes you just have to wave bye-bye in the rear view mirror and go on ahead to make the future," he counseled.

II
Fairfax, Marin County, California
Earlier that morning

"Those bastards," Hank huffed, "are not graffiti artists. They're just lame little thugs."

He and Joan stood in the side parking lot of the old health food store in Fairfax, inspecting the mural. It was a bright seven thirty in the morning. They'd come in over the hill for the treat of coffee at Java Sluts, a local alternative to Starbucks. Joan was rushing off to Oakland to join the protest in front of Citigen, the murderous genetics giant in the East Bay.

"Hank, I don't like it either. Vedana Shiva is one of my heroes too. I'm just saying that kids are gonna express themselves and being a graffiti artist, or trying to be one, is just a way of doing it. Hell, at least they aren't in some gang in the canal shooting each other."

Joan liked Hank a lot. More than like, she reflected. She loved the guy. He had his ranching family background though and was a little rough around the edges. Endearing really.

"It's not just vandalism," Hank continued. "It's political."

Joan studied the rough white dialogue bubble painted over Vedana's head. "Better Dead Than Fed," it read.

Vedana Shiva was one of the patron saints in the popular resistance to gene modification corporations like Monsanto. She had helped raise public awareness in India and abroad about the cynical corporate grab for control of world food production. Her mighty struggle in India, resisting against all odds the planting of GMO crops, had been largely successful.

Joan loved her quote: "GMO stands for God Move Over.". Vedana was inspiring.

"What do you mean, political?" she asked.

Hank tore his eyes away from the defaced mural and met her gaze. Her pretty face calmed him down. "Oh, you remember, about four years ago. That huge typhoon that ripped up Eastern India? The government was about to ignore their own laws and bring in GMO soy and rice to feed people. Vedana organized against it and they dropped the idea. Somehow, they were able to find enough non-Frankenfood after that. Big surprise."

Hank smiled with satisfaction, remembering that victory. Then his face darkened. "That "Better Dead Than Fed" line was what the corporations and their stooges in government came up with after a lot of people died of starvation. It wasn't because no food was available, but that's what they tried to make it sound like. It was because they couldn't distribute what they had efficiently."

Joan nodded, "I remember. They blamed the delay on Vedana Shiva and her organization. Said their resistance jammed up the aid pipeline."

"Yeah," Hank scowled. "Same old horseshit from the people who gave us the war in Iraq."

Joan wasn't certain she understood the causal link, but nodded in agreement anyways. Hank sometimes made inference leaps she couldn't quite follow, but she knew his heart was in the right place.

After coffee, Hank followed her back out to her green Subaru Forester.

"Bye!" she waved. "See you back at the house tonight."

Hank stood on the corner in the warm sun and put out his thumb. He enjoyed hitching back home, up Sir Francis Drake

Boulevard and into the San Geronimo Valley. It was such a precious place. The low mountains that separated the valley from East Marin were "just high enough" he would say. Going west from Fairfax, up and over White's Hill, was to drop into another, better world. The mad hubbub of the San Francisco Bay Area fell away, and the sweet fields and streams and redwoods welcomed him home.

Hank Meyer was proud of his family. The Meyers had been a part of the West Marin scene for over a hundred years. The big ranch had been sold off before Hank was born, but the family home in Lagunitas was still the crown jewel of the valley, at least as far as Hank was concerned. In his backyard the original spring the settlers used still bubbled pure water off the Mt. Barnaby watershed. Even in dry years it flowed steady and true. He loved bending down and drinking that cool water right from the source. It was like kissing Mother Earth.

Hank was proud of his family's early environmental work as well. They were the original ecologists, people who understood the land and how to use it. His father George had helped lead the charge to halt the mindless development that had despoiled East Marin. It was his turn now, to protect West Marin. The forces of greed were never very far away. With environmental battles the good guys only need to lose once and something beautiful gets swept away forever.

"Hello Tokey!" Hank gave the old hound a scratch behind the ears on his way up to the house. "Come on then. Come on, boy!" Tokey smiled his sweet, old dog smile, climbing the steps. He wasn't a puppy anymore but when you raise a dog up from the start, you can always see the puppy in there. "That's right. Come on. Let's go get a drink."

They walked out back together and had a long drink at the spring. Hank's red beard dripped with water. He liked the lumberjack reflection looking back at him from the little pool below the outflow.

After his discharge from the Air Force he'd come back home in time to bury his dad. George hadn't lived long after the cancer claimed his mom. "Oh well, son," dad smiled, "Without my darlin' I just don't feel much like being around here anymore. You're well launched. I like your little gal too. This place needs young hands. It's yours now, in any way that really counts." He died before the end of April. Hank and Joan saw to it that it was a proper sendoff and the effort drew them closer together than ever. That was three years ago now. How time flies!

"OK, old Toke, you lie down for a while and take it easy." Hank smiled down into the rheumy eyes of the old hound. "I've got some adjustments to make on Mr. Lynas."

His workshop was in its own building, a ways up the hill. Hank was glad of that. It kept all the components of Mr. Lynas far away from the main house and Joan. She didn't know about Mr. Lynas and Hank wanted to keep it that way. "Plausible deniability," they called it in the service.

He walked up the hill, unlocked the door to the workshop, flipped on the light and then turned the deadbolt shut once he was inside. Mr. Lynas lay in a locked metal chest across the room. He retrieved the chest key from under his ceramic Snoopy doghouse on the shelf.

The detonator mechanism was pretty simple. As a mechanic in the Air Force Hank had learned all about the basic electronics that hold our modern lives together. The cheap little cell phone had its alarm function, a thin set of wires ran from the vibrator circuit to the C-4 detonator pack. Not rocket science, really. He'd chosen to go with the alarm timer rather than a call up trigger. Accidental wrong number call at the wrong time and Mr. Lynas would miss his target. People could be hurt.

Hank was pleased with himself in securing the C-4. When he'd stashed thirty pounds of the stuff back at the base, he wasn't quite sure what use it would be. Sure, he enjoyed going out into the desert and blowing things up. Who didn't? But Joan's commitment to fighting the corporate grab for life, their "playing God" as she called it, had become his cause too. "She's more of a Christian than me," he thought as he worked on the bomb case. "Took the Ten Commandments to heart. Well, we shall not kill. But we will certainly deal the corporate types a hit. They hate losing money," Hank smiled to himself.

The God argument was weak and he listened patiently when people unpacked it in discussion. In the Air Force he'd had plenty of science, and a broader education to go with it. "If God had wanted us to fly, he'd have given us wings." That old saw was kicked around humorously at the academy. The memory of crusty old Captain Williams weighing in one day in the middle of a lecture on aerodynamics. "Well, God didn't give us wings. But he gave us brains so we could give ourselves wings." Made sense to Hank.

Joan was a true believer, like Vedana, that GMOs were both morally and ethically wrong. Hank wasn't worried about usurping the turf of some deity. What made sense to him was the good old human race just didn't have the basic wisdom needed to do that kind of tinkering. Environmental activists had to be fighting on both the macro and micro fronts. Save a rainforest only to see it decimated by some lab created disease meant to kill plant parasites. "Whoops! Sorry! We didn't mean to do that!"

Like a few years back, the Monsanto people thought they were so clever to engineer BT, a bacterial insecticide into corn. Yeah, it was deadly to the corn borer beetle. It worked. But the pollen from the corn drifted on to nearby milkweed. A whole migration of Monarch butterflies stopped to feed on the milkweed and dropped dead. Nice job, Monsanto. The whole history of GMO was a bunch of guys in white lab coats looking at a disaster they caused and saying, "Gee whiz, didn't expect that one."

He and Joan were a good team. She was bright and beautiful and passionate, giving her time and her love. "Face it," he reflected. "You've hitched your star to hers. We're in this together, and for the long haul." Protecting the environment was a family tradition. Keep Marin GMO free.

Hank hoisted the Igloo Ice Chest on to the counter and began duct taping the C-4 blocks along the bottom. "Low and packed tight. Layer of foil, then the ice bags, soft drinks and sandwiches."

Larry Burnam would deliver Mr. Lynas to Citigen. His job as the night janitor gave him perfect access at the right time. Hank liked Larry. He was a real EarthFirster. Not like that turncoat in England. It had been Larry's idea to call the device "Mr. Lynas", after Mark Lynas. That guy took the cake. Spent years as a real Eco-activist, ripping up, burning GMO test plots in England and elsewhere. Good speaker too. Mark Lynas brought a lot of people on board the struggle. Then that day in Cambridge when he got up and said, "Guess what! I've been doing my homework, looking at the science and I want to apologize. I've been wrong. GMO technology is our best hope moving forward. Organic gardening just isn't going to feed the world."

What a traitor! Larry was blown away, claimed that the industrial political complex had got to him somehow. Threatened him or bought him maybe. "You just don't go from being a mover and shaker in EarthFirst! to wearing a tie and serving as the new mealy-mouthed apologist for the GMO exploiters!" he declared.

No, he and Larry were going to deliver Mr. Lynas back to them.

It will be quite a statement, Hank reflected. At three o'clock in the morning, this coming weekend, Citigen gets vaporized.

Larry knew the layout. Early Sunday morning the only people on campus will be the guards in the cement bunker at the front gate. That will protect their sorry asses, even if they do work for Dr. Frankenstein.

Hank looked down at the ice chest. It was an elegant job, even if he did say so himself. Next Saturday, he'll set the alarm on the cellphone, Larry will pick up the ice chest and wheel it in on his shift. Adíos Citigen. Neat and clean. Maybe next we'll do the O'Shaughnessy Dam. Restore the Hetch Hetchy!

III
Oakland, California
Citigen Corporation

"That's a neat trick!"

Kyle Hoffman grinned at his tech partner, Julie Newsom.

"It's what Dr. Keller called a Trojan Horse. We can link the *Rhizobium* genome to this so the nodules become self-inoculating."

"So," Kyle mused, "you get the nodule induced on the corn roots or the wheat roots inoculated as it forms. I like it."

Julie smiled back and nodded. "And each successive crop builds up the soil with both native *rhizobacterium* and junior here."

She circled the protein structure rotating on her laptop screen. It really was a neat solution. The proposed *rhizobacter* was an exact copy of the naturally occurring form except for the splice-in head protein. Once the root nodule formed it detached like a ship leaving a pier. Instant legume nodule formation with nitrogen fixation benefitting your target crop.

Kyle and Julie were a good team. The fact that their projects were overlapping but not competitive allowed them both the freedom to share and delight in each other's insights.

"How's it going with *Arabidopsis*?" Julie asked.

It was Kyle's turn to shine.

"Good, really good. We used GOD to find the sequence for the histone deacetylase within the genome. Maybe we can use your Trojan Horse to link it into our root exudates."

Kyle metacognitively listened to himself as he spoke to Julie. It was difficult to explain his work to laymen, like the protestors. A fair amount of his mental relaxation time went into the effort. How would he have explained it to the blond woman this morning? "Well Joan, you and I actually agree here. Using glycocides, like the old Roundup weed killer, are just stop-gap measures. I agree with you that creating food crops that can tolerate a monthly drenching of herbicide is not the best plan. It's a losing battle anyway. The weeds get better at beating Roundup every year. In another decade we'll be almost right back at the starting line. What I'm working on is another approach. Lots of plants release chemicals from their roots that suppress the germination and growth of competitors. It's a natural defense strategy. Creating a place in the sun is a very old battle. A little plant I'm working with, a type of mustard called *Arabidopsis*, has this ability to inhibit the growth of nearby plants of other species. I want to find a way to give this ability to plants we want for food. We don't need to kill the competition, just keep them from taking over. And you can see that this would mean the millions of gallons of herbicides being sprayed over the fields would be unneeded."

Kyle glanced up at Julie who was smiling at him.

"Lost in thought?"

He nodded.

"I was just thinking about how to make what we do here accessible, understandable to the public."

"Ah," Julie nodded, "I heard from Cheryl about your water cooler chat with Dave this morning."

Kyle grinned sheepishly and she went on. "I really admire your determination to educate the people at the gate. How do you think it's going?"

Kyle shrugged and stared down at the dancing molecular

structures on the monitor. "I keep trying to find the common ground. Look, if both of our projects are realized, farmers will be able to vastly reduce fertilizer and herbicide use. That's one of the things we all seem to want. That's the real meaning of sustainable."

Julie watched him in silence. Kyle heaved his shoulders and sighed. "Honestly, it reminds me of trying to talk with the Jehovah's Witness people who'd come to the door when I was a kid. They weren't interested in a real discussion. They were just witnessing, putting it out. It was circular, hermetic."

"I know what you mean," Julie nodded, "but you have been invited back on to Science Friday. NPR has a big audience."

Kyle did his "aw shucks" grin. She loved his bashful nature. It wasn't an act. In fact, she was coming to terms in herself with loving more than that. Kyle Hoffman was in his early thirties, hazel blue eyes, straight, sandy blond hair. His face and hands were lean and elegant, sort of Nordic but without the icy distance she often felt from those northern cousins. He was a head taller than her. She liked that too.

"Well the Science Friday stuff is something I like doing. And, yeah, it's a bigger audience. All the hate mail I got last time was hard. I wish people who like things were as vocal about it as the people who hate things."

Julie leaned over and bumped his shoulder with hers. "I thought you were marvelous! Articulate, passionate, clear as a bell. You'll knock 'em dead again next Friday."

"Well I won't mention the GOD again, that's for certain."

The technological heart of Citigen was the Genomic Ontogenesis Device, a true state of the art instrument that could decode strands of nucleic acid, identify, sequence and synthesize. A skilful operator could type a gene sequence out on the keyboard, along with any additions desired, and produce a useful quantity within an hour. The GOD machine could do in a few hours what it had taken the Human Genome Project years to accomplish with painstaking lab work.

It was Kyle's little aside on his last Science Friday appearance that had drawn the ire of so many. Referring to a promising gene therapy on insulin, Kyle had slipped into the jocular language of the lab and called the process a "gift from GOD". In the liberal academic air of the San Francisco Bay Area it was all too easy to forget that large parts of the country took their God story deadly seriously. The death threats that flooded in were a grim reminder of the discouraging polarizations that seemed to divide people from each other these days. A spiritual teacher friend had recently returned from a trip to Israel on which he talked and meditated with groups of Israelis and Palestinians. "People are loyal to their suffering," he had remarked.

Maybe Dave Davenport was right. The Jehovah's Witnesses weren't interested in an exchange of ideas. It seemed like the passionately committed to any ideology had impenetrable blinders preventing contradictory views from coming into the light of awareness. But Kyle also knew it was never a hundred percent. When he was a kid, the anti-communist politicians had an uncompromising article of faith: no communist government would ever cede power in a democratic or popular process. Then the Berlin wall went down and Gorbachev disbanded the Soviet Union and democracy broke out all over Eastern Europe. And someone like Mark Lynas, the activist he cited his last turn on the Science Friday show, was able to move from EarthFirst Eco-terrorism into acceptance, even endorsement, of GMOs as part of the solution to Earth's ills. There was hope.

Kyle put his hand on Julie's. Her skin was warm and soft. "Thanks for your vote of confidence. And for your blessing on talking about your team's work on nitrogen fixation."

Julie flipped her hand so that Kyle's rested in hers. She

intertwined her fingers with his. "Well Dr. Hoffman, if we're going to save the world we'd better get back to work."

IV
Northeastern Pacific
US Coastguard Rescue Mission, C-27 J Spartan
Aircraft, 9,000 ft.

"Ever seen anything like this, Tom?"

The pilot, Tom Brecken, shook his head from side to side. A definite "No".

Below them the sea appeared as a near solid carpet of black. A few breaks caused by currents reflected the afternoon light. It resembled black land crisscrossed by a few lakes and rivers.

"Nope. It's got to be some kind of algae bloom, like a red tide. Except maybe a black tide."

"The carbon monoxide levels down there are deadly." Jim, his longtime co-pilot, was examining the readouts from the sniffer and satellite feeds that NOAA had hurriedly fitted to the big surveillance plane.

"We should be within visual of the Maersk ship in the next few minutes."

Late yesterday afternoon the emergency ops had received a panicked SOS from some poor sucker out in the middle of this. He was breathing on a scuba tank and reported the entire crew dead from asphyxiation. Jim hoped he had more than one tank available.

"Contact. There she is."

Tom adjusted the heading one degree to the west. From nine thousand feet the ship looked good. The *Kentang* was on a straight heading, a churning white wake behind. But the black mat over the sea and the dark haze in the air was anomalous, industrial somehow. Like some disaster in an oil field.

"I'm going to take her down slowly. You tell me when," Tom said.

Other rescue craft were on their way to rendezvous with the container ship. This mission was to determine the vertical distribution of the carbon monoxide and relay safe perimeter coordinates to the others. The claxon aboard the big aircraft notified all crew to don oxygen masks. Tom and Jim fitted their masks and they began the slow descent.

External readings were normal down to about five thousand feet. Then the sniffer started clicking up. "What do you have?" Tom asked at four thousand.

"We've gone to point zero zero one two. Now one three."

At point zero zero seven, Tom had orders to halt descent and head east to determine horizontal horizon. The rescuers would have to hold off at point zero zero five, and even that was pushing it. They'd have to wait for the *Kentang* to come to them.

They were about to pass over the Maersk ship at two thousand feet when Jim said, "That's it." Tom pulled back on the yoke and banked starboard, onto a due east flight path. He brought it back up to twenty five hundred. There was no sign of life on the container ship.

"Relay that data to radio. Notify when external drops to point zero zero five."

The National Security Cutter *Kimball* was on a western intercept with the *Kentang*. They had a Dolphin chopper on the rear deck and planned to land a team with closed rebreathers on the pad of the ship when they were within range. The Dolphin had a halfway range of about a hundred and forty miles so the plan was to get close enough without asphyxiating everybody aboard.

Tom kept the plane at twenty five hundred. Finally, Jim said what he wanted to hear. "Levels are dropping. Point zero zero five."

The black algae or whatever it was seemed to be thinning out as well. More open water between shrinking, floating mats of the stuff.

Tom descended, following the diminishing concentration level down. At a hundred and twelve miles from the *Kentang* the black mats were nearly absent. They were four hundred feet above the surface when Jim said, "External CO level at point zero zero two and dropping."

"Contact the *Kimball* with our position," he said. "Here's their staging point."

V
Coos Bay, Oregon
Randall Clinic

Dr. Terrence Randall was justifiably proud of his practice. Over the last twenty-four years his small, country doctor's office had grown into a fine regional care facility. Their cardiac unit received higher ratings than any hospital in the southern Willamette Valley, and they were the go-to emergency and ICU center for fifty miles along the Oregon coast. His practice included three other full time MDs and nearly a dozen nurse practitioners.

"Good afternoon, Dr. Randall." Kelly Sheehan gave him her gorgeous red headed, big lipped smile.

"Hi Kelly. I didn't know you were in today."

"Oh," Kelly demurred for a moment then spoke again. "I'm standing in for Linda. Her little boy got banged up in a tricycle accident and she's home with him."

"A tricycle accident?" Dr. Randall's eyebrows went up a notch. "I guess things are getting rough out there on the kindergarten commute," he smiled. "He's not too bad I hope?"

"Oh no," Kelly reassured him. "Just a scuff on the cheek when the front wheel fell off. More hurt pride than anything else, but you know Linda."

He nodded. Yes, he knew Linda. She was as fine a nurse as he'd ever known, but, as a mom, maybe a bit over weaning.

"Well, they don't build 'em like they used to, eh? One of those plastic trikes from China I'll bet."

"Where else!" laughed Kelly.

He liked her spunk and full figure. It had been almost seven years now since he'd lost Margaret. Kelly was fetching, but he'd learned a long time ago that you don't start intimate relationships with someone who works for you. Just the power difference made it unethical. And other factors. Still, as Kelly swayed off down the hall it was with some effort that he pulled his eyes back to the med chart in his hands.

Terrence pushed through the double doors of the ICU and made his way past four unoccupied beds to the far end of the unit. The patient in the fifth bed turned his head to smile.

"Hello Art. How's the arm feeling today?"

Arthur Cribb was originally from England and still retained the genteel air of a country squire. Thirty-two years as a lumberjack had roughened his hands but not his spirit. He joked that he never thought the trees would go away before he did. Now, four years into his forced retirement, he carved wooden children's toys and had quite a following.

"Good afternoon, Doctor. Oh, better than yesterday. I can flex my fingers without pain. That's good, isn't it?"

"Yes, really very good. Multiple breaks like this can take quite some time to mend. The blood loss and sepsis is really our biggest concern, but you're doing quite well there too."

He walked around the bed and tapped at the hanging bag of glucose saline. The drip tube led into Art's unbroken left arm. "Who was on janitorial this week?" he thought. The black grit on the bag and the IV tube looked unprofessional. He didn't want to start yelling in front of Art so he came back around and looked over the chart. He smiled down at the older man.

"I'll check back with you in a few minutes. I need to speak with Melissa at the nursing station."

Art nodded and smiled weakly. "She's a good one, that Melissa. I feel like a baby when she rolls me over."

"Back in a moment," he said, and moved down the row of beds to the nursing station.

"Can we have a word in the hall?" he asked.

Melissa looked up, prepared to smile, but the expression in his eyes shut her down. "Of course," she replied guardedly and moved out the door.

Once in the hall, Dr. Randall tightly hissed, "What the hell is going on with the IV drip bag and line for Mr. Cribb? It's filthy, covered with oily grit of some kind."

Melissa's eyes grew wide and she stammered, "I don't know. I don't know what you mean. It was all perfectly clean when I changed it out this morning, just before lunch."

Dr. Randall held her in his fierce stare for a moment but relented. There had to be an explanation. He knew Melissa to be competent and attentive.

"Alright. Let's go look together. Don't say anything that might alarm Mr. Cribb. We'll just switch it out like a normal procedure. Let's go."

Melissa secured a Steripack from the cabinet, a new, bagged saline/glucose, and followed behind.

"Hello Art. We're back. Just a little discussion with Melissa about the best course for you. We're going to change the irrigation bag and line for now."

Art nodded and closed his eyes, apparently exhausted. Dr. Randall moved around the bed to the metal pole. The IV bag was coated with some sort of oily looking black soot. "What is this?" he said quietly, almost to himself, and ran a finger down the bag, tracing the greasy film. The bag split open, as though his finger was a scalpel. The fluid burst out and over Mr. Cribb's left shoulder and face. The cold shock caused the old man to bolt upright, his shattered right arm and shoulder jerked along. Mr. Cribb screamed in pain, as if he were being killed.

Dr. Randall glared at the ruptured bag. "What the hell is going on?" he asked aloud.

VI
Northeastern Pacific
Aboard the National Security Cutter, *Kimball*

Charlie Baskin had a giddy sense of déjà vu. The white walls of the infirmary, the oxygen mask. But there was the reassuring difference of a living being smiling down at him. It was a kind face, but not one he recognized.

"Welcome back to the world of the living, Mr. Baskin."

The last Charlie could recall was painfully wrestling the oxygen tank from the welder's corner in the ship workshop up to the infirmary and Mickey Mousing a connection to the medical regulator of his mask. It was hard to do with raw, bleeding hands. In the seven hours since he got through to the Coast Guard, all they could tell him on the radio was that help was on the way. A parade of talkers asked him about the ship, what he saw, what did he think was going on. At one point he got angry.

"I don't know what the hell is going on. The ocean is covered with some kind of black crud, the goddamned air is poisonous, everybody and everything I see aboard is dead. Don't ask me to fucking explain it to you. God Damn it, get out here!"

But their ETA wasn't until midmorning tomorrow. They were doing their best, they said, but they had to do it right or more people would die.

Charlie'd already gone through four of the scuba tanks talking on the radio from the bridge. He had to preserve the last two tanks. They were his only means of moving around the ship. Reluctantly, he'd signed off.

Now, back in the infirmary, he was drawing on the face mask and the big green tank. By ten o'clock the gauge was down to six, down from the fifteen when he'd turned it off this morning and moved to the scuba. He'd used it at a rate of about one and a half per hour. Charlie felt his guts churning. The oxygen he had would be exhausted by two o'clock in the morning. He had searched the infirmary and surrounding storage. There was no second tank. That suggestion would go on the note to Maersk they'd find around his suffocated neck. The only other oxygen on the ship was down in the workshop level, part of the welder's rig. There was nothing for it. Better to try and breathe welding oxygen than keel over dead. Hell, maybe it was so contaminated it would kill him.

After he got the welding tank up to the infirmary he went back down for another scuba regulator and a tool kit. The medical regulator was a different connection set up, but it looked like the valve from the scuba would fit the welding tank. With some spare parts and a bit of finesse Charlie was able to fabricate a workable connection between the tank and the medical regulator. His vision was jumpy, his breathing rough. He'd never felt so exhausted in his life.

Here goes. He turned the valve on the welding tank. No leak. Then he turned the valve on the regulator. The pressure gauge shot up to a bit over thirty.

Charlie staggered removing the scuba outfit, but steadied himself on the bed and fitted the mask in place. He breathed. The oxygen was flowing. He secured the head straps in place and sat down on the bed, then laid back into a deep and dreamless sleep.

"Welcome back to the world of the living, Mr. Baskin."

Charlie blinked away the memory and the blackness.

"Nice to be back," he croaked, voice dry and ragged. "Thirsty."

Charlie raised a hand and noticed his bandages had been replaced.

"Sure thing. We'll have that right here."

The uniformed man with the kind face handed him a plastic bottle with a flexible straw.

"Just a moment, here. Lean your head up a bit. I'll get this mask off so you can drink easier."

Charlie looked around the room and three other friendly faces nodded to him. One wore a white commander's uniform. With the mask laid aside, he took a long drink of the sweet, salty mix. "Gatorade or something," he thought.

The man in the officer's uniform stood nearer the bed and gazed down at him warmly. "That was pretty good, that set-up you rigged with the oxygen tank. You saved yourself."

Charlie nodded, acknowledging the compliment, but asked, "Everybody?"

The officer's face clouded. "Yup. Except for you. It was a ghost ship when we got there."

A fit of coughing reminded Charlie that he was still damaged goods and the Doc helped slip the mask back in place. He spoke sympathetically, "I reckon you're tired of this, but it saved your life. We'll get you to the mainland. They'll be able to work better with the burns than we're set up for here. Just rest now."

The assembled men nodded to him and departed the room.

The doctor said, "I'll be back in a minute with some food for you. How does a cheese omelette sound?"

Charlie managed a smile inside the mask. His voice cracked, "It sounds good."

July 19th

I
Oakland, California
Citigen

"Why you specifically?" Julie asked. There was no envy or ill will in her question. She felt pleased that NOAA had sent a sample from the Gyre rescue to Citigen for analysis and evaluation. She was simply curious and a bit surprised that they had asked for Kyle, for Dr. Hoffman, to head up the investigative team.

Kyle grinned and ran a hand back through his hair. "They said because of my work on marine fungi at UC. I had co-authorship on a fair number of the papers out of Samuelson's lab. With him gone, I guess they thought I was the next best thing to a real expert."

Julie smiled back at him and inclined her cover girl perfect face and neck to best effect. "So, they've ID'd Boogie as a fungi, not an algae like everybody thought at first?" She used the name for the organism that the Coast Guard Science Officer had used when he talked about it. When the rescue team had landed on the Maersk ship the C.O. had radioed back that it looked like the Boogieman had come aboard. Everyone and everything dead. No sign of violence or struggle. They all just stopped and dropped where they stood. The crew aboard the *Kimball* had begun referring to the algal samples they brought back as "Boogie" and the name stuck.

Kyle shook his head affirmatively at Julie's inquiry. "That's right. The guys in the rescue helicopter described a mat on the surface of the water they thought was black algae. The lab in Seattle that received the first samples figured out immediately that it was multicellular but not photosynthetic." They looked into the saltwater isolation aquarium on the lab bench. The floating mass did resemble a clump of blue-green algae, almost like the mats of cyanobacter you'd see in some estuary zones of the San Francisco Bay.

Kyle indicated a stereoscope beside the tank. "Have a look. You can see pretty clearly that the black velvet component is conidia."

Julie peered into the scope and adjusted the fine focus. "Conidia. That's the spore producing part?"

"Yeah. You see how it looks like little branches with the round spores coming off the end, like a string of pearls?"

"Uh-huh," she said, and used the stage dials to slightly shift the view of the slide. "So the mass that looks like clear spaghetti at the bottom, that's the main body?"

"I think so," Kyle ventured. "Usually you don't see a mycelium in a free floating marine fungi. I don't know of any. Normally a mycelium would be invested in a substrate, like a piece of floating wood or the like," he added.

"You mean like how a bread mold works its way through a loaf?"

"Exactly. And without a microscope you don't even know it's there until it puts up a fruiting body. You remember *Rhizopus*, with the little stalks that looked like black dandelions? Spore dispersal is the name of the game." Kyle bent down to counter height and gazed intently at the floating mass. "What's strange about Boogie here is that he is putting up a fruiting body that's more like an *Ascomycetes*."

Julie wanted to tussle his hair. It was weird, childish. She wanted his attention on her, not the glop in the tank. But she restrained her hand and asked a question instead.

"So not *Zygomycetes*, bread mold family?"

"No, huh-uh," Kyle replied distractedly. "More like a yeast. But what is the nutrient substrate? Yeasts will eat a carbohydrate and give off carbon dioxide, just like we do. Boogie is giving off carbon monoxide, or so we think." He tapped the sensor array attached to the aquarium. "And right now, not even that."

Julie came around beside Kyle and rested her chin on her hands, peering in at the fungal mass. "What did the GOD sequencing come up with? Is this somebody new?"

Kyle nodded. "It's not in the marine fungi database. The closest DNA match was terrestrial, a fungi associated with tree roots called *Neolecta*, but nowhere close enough to be a direct relation."

"Why no evidence of metabolic activity right now?" she asked.

Kyle shrugged. "Nothing to eat."

II
Lagunitas , West Marin, California

"Hank, you might be my brother-in-law pretty soon so that's why I'm putting this out to you and Joan. It's a ground floor opportunity."

Joan shook her head ruefully, looking at her brother across the table. He'd always been like that, making assumptions, embarrassing people. She and Hank didn't have anything formally agreed upon. Having her brother's "bull in a china shop" approach to human relationships there made her cringe.

There was a sharpness in her voice when she spoke. "Perry, you're not a scientist. You're a medical supplies distributor. Besides, if this is so great, why in Mexico? Why not just open in California?"

"Little sister, you are an accomplished programmer. Down the road I'd love to have your skills on our website. But you are not a business person."

Joan's older brother winked at Hank. He had her blond hair and green eyes, but where Joan's nose was petite above well-formed lips he had a potato of a schnoz that reminded Hank of W.C. Fields. He was fleshy cheeked and admitted to loving good California wine. Perhaps "to an excess from time to time" he would joke.

Perry leaned in over the plates, the remains of their lunch on the patio attracting a few yellow jackets. "Trying to get this off the ground in California's regulatory environment would be virtually impossible," he explained. "In Mexico we've got top talent from the medical schools in Guadalajara. Most of our lead team members are doctoral graduates from the US. The Ponce de Leon Clinic has been up and running for nearly four years. We wouldn't have even been to the proposal review stage in California."

Joan snorted. "That's because it's too creepy, Perry."

Hank caught Perry's eye. "Perry, when you speak about getting in on the ground floor I'm uncertain why you'd need my investment. It sounds to me like you've already got a stable full of wealthy older people who are benefitting. Why not tap them?"

Perry put on his patient, fatherly face. "That is happening, Hank. I'm coming to you with an offer that could make you a lot of money, a lot more than you'll ever see from that non-profit you're with. We want to keep our investor numbers small and intimate, at least until after the expansion. Also," he chuckled, "you'll be able to take care of my little sister in style."

Hank smiled. "Would that include treatments for us in our golden years?"

"Thinking ahead. I like that," Perry replied. "This would make your golden years golden in more ways than one, Hank. We're talking about living to a hundred, maybe more, and feeling as healthy and as fit as you feel right now."

"It's unnatural," Joan said flatly. "I know it's nothing to do with GMO Frankenscience, Perry. I wouldn't even be sitting here at the table with you if it was. Neither would Hank." She glanced over at him and he nodded approval of her sentiment. "But the Bible says three score and ten. I think anything beyond that is a gift from God."

Perry sighed. "Joan, I love you. But Mom and Dad are almost eighty now. They've had a natural life. You heard Dad though, back at Thanksgiving last year. Now everything feels like it's wearing out. It hurts just to get out of bed. We can fix that."

"I also heard him say no thanks to your fix," she said defiantly.

Sister and brother stared across the chasm at each other.

"How about that, Perry? What's the argument when somebody says it's not natural?" Hank looked at him expectantly.

Perry leaned back in his chair and studied the pair. "Look, for all your life, when you've become ill or injured yourself your body stepped up and fixed itself. Sometimes it needed a little help, like Joan, when you used antibiotics a couple of years back for the bronchial pneumonia. OK, well, when we get older the fix-it system starts to break down. All we're doing at the Ponce de Leon Clinic is fixing the fix-it system," he smiled.

Hank shifted, "OK, fair enough. But the children and the transfusion part. How does that work?"

Perry nodded and winked. That was the right question and he was ready for it.

"Hank, about eight years ago at UC, they hooked up the circulatory system of a young rat to an old rat, so that they shared blood. A remarkable thing happened. The young blood stimulated stem cell formation in the older rat. It was as if they turned back the clock and the older rat's body began to repair itself as if it were a young body. The young blood induced the body of the older rat to regenerate. And it was a lasting change. They found they could dial back the biological age of the older rat to half of its chronological age. The fountain of youth."

"What happened to the young rat?" Joan grumbled.

"That's a point," agreed Perry. "If they left them hooked up, the body of the younger rat began to age more rapidly, almost an exact counter balance to the regeneration of the stem cells in the older rat. It's a factor in the young blood."

"So the children...!" Joan looked stricken, struggling for words.

"No, no, the children are fine," soothed Perry. "What they did in the lab was trade out the young rats. The blood factor wasn't something they could nail down. It's a synergistic effect, not a chemical. So they had a population of forty young rats with the same blood type. Every day they'd swap out for a new subject, and one day in transfusion mode did absolutely no harm to the young rat! The result was that the old rat had its youth and vitality restored at no biological cost to the donor population. We do exactly the same with our youthful donor population."

Hank shook his head at this. "So, in your clinic, you are using this transfusion of young blood into aging people and getting the same result?"

Perry nodded. "Magnificent results in fact. We have clients in their seventies, early eighties who have turned back the clock. After one year of the treatment."

"What!" Joan burst out. "One year!"

Perry seemed genuinely taken aback at her outburst. "Well, yes. Think about your own healing. If you had an accident or a major surgery it might take you six months or a year to get back to normal. We can heal the healing system but it takes a while to dial back all the deteriorating systems associated with old age."

Hank broke in, incredulous. "So your clients have to stay hooked up to the blood of children for a year?"

Perry's eyes widened as he grasped their misunderstanding. "No, no. Sorry! Our clients come in for a one month treatment every six months for two years. Four treatments in total, uh, four months out of twenty four. Our data shows that patients receive the maximum benefit after four treatments. Moving forward, we find that only one treatment a year is needed to maintain the improvement in most subjects."

"What about the children?" Joan asked darkly. "What becomes of them?"

Perry again smiled broadly. "The children are one of our success stories, Joan. Every child admitted to the donor program is restricted to one recipient. Any child in our program only shares blood twice a year. I mean, they aren't giving blood like at a blood bank. They are trading blood. It has virtually no discernable negative impact on the child, but what they receive in return is something we are very proud of.

"Every child in the program receives top quality medical treatment, not just for themselves but for their entire family. Our donor children receive free education through college if they want it, or training in a trade program to learn self-supporting skills. And they are very well paid for their two blood shares per year, more than four thousand dollars at the current exchange rate. For a lot of our families that is a significant part of the total income for the year."

"And the government of Mexico approves this?" Hank asked.

"Well, we're working through a university in Guadalajara. Our treatment center comes under the auspices of a clinical research project. As such, our direct supervision is via the university, not the government per se. The recruitment of donor families is through the research associates at the school. It's all quite on the up and up."

"So," Joan tapped her fingers on the dining table, "you are looking for funds to expand your clinical research project, is that right?"

"That's right. Our clinic currently has a capacity of eighteen patients per month. The plan is to expand to a hundred bed facility by the end of next year." Perry leaned in again, as if sharing an important confidence. "In certain circles, the word is out. We've a waiting list of over twenty-seven hundred people!"

"Twenty-seven hundred!" whistled Hank. "Perry, what does the Ponce de Leon Clinic charge for a one month treatment?"

"Well, bear in mind that it isn't a one month treatment Hank, it's four treatments spread over two years. It currently works out to a little over four hundred thousand US for a treatment. That's considering one million seven hundred thousand for the two year course."

Hank shook his head, "Not a therapy for the poor."

"No Hank. Not a therapy for the poor. But if you're eighty years old and can spend a part of your fortune to be forty again, it's a fair trade. Frankly, for most of our clients it's chump change," Perry said with a wink. "Everybody wins."

Joan pushed away from the table and stood up. "You should change the name to the Count Dracula Clinic! No wonder dad didn't want any part of it. It's… it's … demonic!" she announced and walked out of the room.

Hank and Perry watched her departure.

"Christians," said Perry.

"What sort of return would I be looking at for an investment of two hundred thousand?" asked Hank.

III
Lincoln City, Oregon Coast

"Do you like the black one or the blue one?"

Len glanced absently at the two rubbish bins. "It will be under the sink, Sharon. I don't give a damn what color it is. We won't see it."

"You'll see it when you take it out," she remonstrated.

Phil Gayette looked on, impassive. He'd taken the floor job at Plastic World as a summer job. He'd finished High School in May and wasn't quite sure what was next. Maybe college. His mom had said, "Get a job or get movin."

Now he presided over his kingdom of plastic buckets, laundry baskets, storage containers, you name it. If the Chinese could make it out of plastic, you'd find it at Plastic World. Neon greens, fluorescent oranges, good solid reds and blues, all the colors of the rainbow. The children's toy section was more colorful than the cereal aisle at Safeway.

He looked over and she was still there, the filthy broken tricycle in the middle of the walkway. He was relieved that Benjamin, the store owner, had come out of the office at exactly the right moment. Now he had to deal with her.

"Well look at it!" she almost shrieked. "My little boy could have been killed if this defective piece of junk fell apart coming down our hill."

"Mrs. Martinez, I completely understand and of course, we'll fully refund you."

Ben had a good bedside manner with difficult customers.

This was the third time in as many weeks Phil had watched him defuse irate buyers. Telling them to go fuck themselves was not an option if he wanted to keep the job, so he listened surreptitiously and learned.

"Honestly, we have not seen this problem with any of the Monster Trykes. I will certainly be in touch with the distributor about it."

He bent down and poked at the mounting forks. They had failed, causing the front wheel to detach. The plastic was softened and blackened. It reminded him of how DEET, the mosquito repellent, would eat some plastics.

Mrs. Martinez stared at Ben, mollified but not done.

"It's lucky that I'm a nurse. I was right there. It took me half an hour to stop his poor little forehead bleeding. He got a bad scuff on the asphalt."

Ben nodded sympathetically as he straightened himself.

"I have two boys myself, Mrs. Martinez. I know exactly how you feel. Here, let me take this in back. If you'll go over to the cashier, I'll be there in a moment." Ben lifted both parts of the broken toy and moved towards the warehouse. When he dropped it inside, just past the swinging doors, he almost unconsciously brushed the greasy, black mess coating his hands on his pant leg. "Better not," he thought. Instead he stepped over to the little sink that served the restroom. It washed off easily enough. Some kind of road treatment?

"We'll take the blue one," Sharon said. Her comment pulled Phil back to the pair in front of him. He nodded and picked up the can to take it over to the cashier for them. "I'd like a new one please," she said. "That one's all greasy."

Phil looked at his hand. Sure enough, an oily dark film where he'd touched the can. "OK, no problem. I understand." He went back to the stack and pulled a nice clean one out of the middle. "Here you are. Thanks for coming in."

"Len, you take it," she said. "I want to go next door and get some of those cute dish towels. I'll meet you at the car." With that she turned and swished out. Her ivory summer dress brushed against the plastic flower garlands adorning the front door. Phil noticed the long, black streaks that suddenly marred the fabric. Len didn't seem to notice. He paid and trudged joylessly out towards the parking lot.

Phil approached the door and ran his hand over the red plastic poinsettias. It came away greasy and blackened.

IV
Brookings, Oregon Coast
Thomas Creek Bridge

Bobby flipped on the emergency flashers and tucked the little truck as close in to the curb as he could. This stretch of Highway 101 wasn't too busy in the morning. Most of the tourists heading north or south wanted to be over on I-5 where they could really make some time. Still, there was enough traffic that he wanted to get the gear unloaded and his truck off the bridge as quickly as possible.

He and Tim jumped out first. Randy, sandwiched into the little, rear bench seat, took a bit longer to extricate himself. He wasn't fat exactly, but his center of gravity made the angle of exit awkward.

The three boys hoisted the harness and bungee cord assembly out of the back of the truck in one smooth lift and settled in on the walkway. All three took a moment to gaze down the three hundred and forty-five feet to the small creek below. The Thomas Creek Bridge was the highest span in Oregon and a favorite for bungee jumpers from all over the Pacific Northwest. It was technically illegal. The State Police would likely give them more than a warning if a patrol came by in the middle of things, but life was full of risk. Both Bobby and Tim had jumped the Thomas recently and Randy was keen on being part of the club. When he looked down he felt a little twist in his guts. This was higher than anything he'd ever done. But the moment passed and he stood with Tim while Bobby pulled the truck down to the turnout at the south end of the bridge.

"Let's check over the harness," Tim suggested.

The two began fitting the straps for Randy. Bobby came back, nodded approvingly, then set to work getting the recovery pulley attached to the bridge railing. Bobby smiled, "It's a good day Randy. Not too hot with the clouds."

Temperature was important. The bungee cord, multiple latex lines encased in a stressed polypropylene sleeve, would stretch farther if it was too hot. Of course, the sheath would prevent any catastrophic overstretch, but it was a rough stop if the jumper was going too fast. The art was to have the latex lines slow the last part of the fall completely and avoid the vicious jerk of the sleeve. It was all by the chart, but environmental factors made it less exact. In general, cooler was better.

Randy stood at the railing, looking down. He gave a startled jerk when a passing logging truck gave him twin blasts on the big air horn. The driver waved him a thumbs up. Randy smiled and returned the gesture. He always had a few butterflies before a jump. His last jump with Bobby had been over a hundred feet.

"Hell," Bobby had said, "people break their necks falling off a three foot step ladder. After the first twenty feet it doesn't matter how high you are. Longer is better because of the bounce."

Randy watched as Bobby and Tim secured the bungee and began to feed the line over the railing. He'd have a maximum three hundred foot extension on his farthest excursion, still fifty feet above the creek.

The bunched-up sock of the polypropylene sheath didn't lend itself well to sliding over the railing, so it was a hand-over-hand process feeding it down that reminded Randy of the TV ad for the miracle hose that never got tangled. There it was, all scrunched together, then somebody would turn on the water and the thing would wriggle like a snake and get all full and stretched out. His brother had said, "That's what my dick does!" and they both laughed and laughed.

"Did you leave this out in the rain?" Tim asked. He was looking at the wet, black residue on his hands.

Bobby shook his head, perplexed. "No, it was in under the shed roof with the rest of the lines."

Bobby rubbed his hands together. "I don't know how it got oily like this."

"What's up?" Randy walked over, looking at the last thirty feet of the line coiled on the cement.

"Line sleeve is sort of wet and gunky," Tim answered.

Randy leaned over and lifted a length of the coil. "This part's dry," he observed.

"I dunno," Bobby said. "Maybe it got splashed on the drive."

Randy looked over the edge. The long dark loop of the line was hanging down almost a hundred feet. Another logging truck roared past. The driver waved and gave a blast on his air horn.

"Let's do this," Randy said decisively.

Tim and Bobby anchored the bungee to the harness with the secondaries around Randy's ankles. They helped him move another ten feet along the span and climb over. The loop was hanging well away. It was a straight shot out and down, no danger of getting entangled on the way.

This was the moment of truth, and the three friends stood in the late morning light. Randy was facing out towards the sea, his arms outstretched behind him, holding the railing. He looked back over his shoulder.

"One small step for man..." he smiled.

"One great leap for bungee!" Tim and Bobby shouted in unison.

Randy leaped straight out. It was a good dive, a good fall line. Tim and Bobby peered over the edge and watched him sail past the bottom of the loop. The line began to stretch and straighten. The latex offered resistance, pulling against his fall.

The polypropylene line was uncrimped, approaching its limit. But Randy kept falling. Bobby involuntarily gripped the railing.

A series of pops, jolts on the cord, the jerking vibration passing through the railing into their hands. "What the fuck!" Tim shouted.

The poly sleeve was fracturing, snapping into smaller sections. Taut grey latex lines sickeningly naked, fraying, retracting.

Their eyes were on Randy, his arms outstretched. He was slowing, but had overshot the line limit. It was way too fast.

Both boys recoiled as Randy impacted headfirst into the stones of the creek bed and started back, the screamingly taut latex lines now drawing him up. A strangled, animal noise escaped from Bobby as Randy's headless torso rose toward them in slow motion. A horrible spray of red from the neck traced an arc in the air as the body whirled and began to descend again, away from them.

V
Canon Beach, Oregon Coast

"Please, daddy?"

Scott put down the paper he was reading to focus on the cherubic cheeks and sweet blond curls. Mina was such a revelation to him. His little girl. It wasn't this way with her older brother. He loved Jimmy to bits, his first born son. Even at eight years old they understood each other as men. There was the tenderness of father and son, but not like Mina. She opened him up, and he was defenseless.

"OK, my little lamb. Let's go see what we can do."

Scott had bought the beach house a year after Mina was born, almost six years ago. It was a great getaway from Beaverton, out of the sprawl, away from the cookie cutter mini malls. Both Karla and he loved the openness and fresh breezes off the sea.

This had been a very decent summer. Today was the first day of rain that they'd had in July, and the month was more than half over. Scott opened the cabinet drawer beside the big plasma screen, extracting the remote. He was not a big fan of children's television, much preferring family time to be more interactive, but Mina loved the Snow Princess stories. He compromised and watched them with her. He barely registered how the DVD case felt oily when he popped it open.

"Here we go," Scott smiled. "Let's see what happens when Princess Lilly meets the polar bear. Oh, hi Jimmy, come on in."

Red haired Jimmy had slipped into the room, looking a bit sullen. "What are you going to watch?" he asked. Scott knew the drill and winked at Jimmy. "Well, I'm going to ask for a rematch on the Grand Prix Racer with you just as soon as we finish the Snow Princess."

Jimmy wasn't fooled, but he was mollified. "OK. Call me when it's over." He walked off into the kitchen.

Scott looked down at the DVD in his hands. The oily, black fingerprints on the disc startled him and he looked at his hands.

"Oh, me and my dirty hands." He picked the wipe rag up off the DVD collection shelf and buffed away the smudges. "Here we go," he smiled at Mina.

When he pressed the green power button the house lights flickered. A loathsome sixty cycle hum erupted from the side of the plasma TV. In an instant he heard the breaker trip in the panel above the cabinet, but the small, blue cloud of smoke rising from the side of the TV made him sick. He was an IT guy. Before he even examined it, he knew the circuit was cooked.

"What's the matter daddy?

"Ooh, honey, I think we blew a fuse."

"What's a fuse?"

"You just sit tight and I'll take a look, OK?"

Karla had come in from the kitchen holding a piece of toast in a napkin. Jimmy peered around from behind her. "We lost the plugs in the kitchen. What happened?"

"I think we had a short circuit over here."

He bent and shifted the plasma display. The TV housing felt oily. Just like the DVD case, he realized. He reached around and grasped the plug to disconnect the set.

"What the hell?"

Karla suddenly looked alarmed. Scott did not swear in front of the children.

"What is it?" she asked, moving closer.

Scott swiveled and held out the cable and plug towards her. It was a gloppy black mess of exposed copper wire. "It's melted," he said wonderingly. "Not from heat. It just melted."

VI
Approaching Portland International Airport
Aboard Alaska Flight 212

Tucker Creed loved flying, ever since he was a kid. He used to clip out the "I Want to Fly a Cessna for Five Dollars" coupon in Life magazine every week and ride his Schwinn bike over to Van Nuys airport.

"Hey," the pilots would laugh. "It's Tucker with another coupon."

The promotion by Cessna to drum up interest in buying a private plane may not have been a great success for the company. At five dollars a shot, it was a great success for Tucker. There wasn't any age limit attached to the offer and it tickled the guys at Cessna that a kid was that keen to fly. After the first few times, they'd take him up for a lot longer than the advertised thirty minute intro flight. He got good enough that they'd let him be at the controls of the little 150 for landings and take-offs. "You're a natural," Buck would laugh. He was the chief teacher at the flight school. Tucker thought he was great.

Now, here he was. A pilot for Alaska Airlines, bringing a 737 into Portland. In his thirty-two years of commercial flight he never lost the joy of swinging the clouds like a bird.

There were clouds aplenty today.

"We've got an IMC alert out of PDX, Tucker."

His co-pilot, Bill, was a good man. He was twenty years younger than Tucker, but they both agreed things were a mess in Washington. Tucker was flying when Ronald Reagan decided to union bust and fired all the air traffic controllers.

"I've heard some of the stories," Bill said. "All the near misses."

"Too much faith in technology," Tucker reflected.

"You need real experience in the plane and on the ground. There's just no substitute for knowing what you're doing."

On this, Bill and Tucker were in lockstep.

As the jet winged north, the cloud cover thickened, cumulus rising along the Cascades to the east. IMC meant Instrument Meteorological Conditions. "And that doesn't mean they're striking up the band," Tucker would invariably joke.

Like it or not, they'd be depending on technology for the landing. Coming in to Portland was a favorite approach, it was a beautifully situated town. From the air, the confluence of the Willamette and the Colombia with Mt. Hood rearing up to the east presented a classic Northwest picture. On some days, depending on the wind, they'd approach from the east, sliding down past Mt. Hood, along the Colombia. But Tucker liked coming in from the coast, flying east and crossing the low coastal range then paralleling the Colombia. That view of Mt. Hood was always a crowd pleaser.

Today the tower was calling for the western approach. In a sense, it was a little easier. With the field socked in Tucker felt the newer ILS system was a better deal, even if he couldn't enjoy the view. After all these years his mental picture of the field was almost like a GPS display. He knew pilots who'd gone in on full autopilot, but that wasn't something he'd ever do at Portland. Get some sudden crosswind and the auto could over compensate the horizontal, end up in the muck. Or the river. Autopilots! It was almost a joke among pilots when that Turkish airliner crashed in Holland a few years back. Their autopilot cut the motors ten meters above the runway because the GPS said they were there. Except that Schiphol airport is below sea level.

When the pilot realized the error he gave the ship too much thrust, which made the nose go up and smashed the tail into the ground. No, if you want to fuck up big, trust a computer.

Tower radioed clearance and they began their approach. It was sunny on the coast at fifteen thousand feet, but soon they were in the soup. The view was a flat grey, it suddenly felt as if they were motionless. Tucker kept the localizer and glide slope displays on both screens.

"Tower is reporting wind shear running north north east across the runway, 40 to 45."

Tucker nodded and allowed himself a little smile. "Well, that's why we are not on autopilot, Bill. Need the hands of a pilot."

The ILS Instrument Landing System had two redundant backups. The two directional radio signals were integrated, but each was transmitted by independent arrays. One set, the localizers, put out the horizontal, and the center line of the runway appeared on the screen running vertically. The other set, the glide slope, sent out a precise pathway leading down to the runway at three percent. Onboard ground sensors and cameras below gave detail, even at one hundred percent loss of visibility. The system was brilliant and reliable. Unless the insulation on the electronics inexplicably liquefied and shorted out the works. At three thirty seven p.m. that's exactly what happened.

"Distance two point four seven, altitude seven oh five. Watch the crosswind, it's kicking up right now."

Tucker compensated and kept the plane exactly centered on the horizontal and vertical signals.

"Gear down," he directed.

At three thirty-six Bill called the approach, "Distance one point four, altitude three hundred."

Tucker lowered the flaps the rest of the way and the big plane slowed noticeably and began to drop into the slot. He was coming in a little fast to cut the crosswinds, but Tucker knew the runway was long enough to run out the speed.

Three thirty-seven. Red lights across the board.

"We've got a failure flag, auto shutdown on ILS," Bill shouted.

"God damn it," Tucker hissed, "Gear up".

Without hesitation he gave the big jet power and pulled back on the yoke, climbing but not too steep. He didn't want to pull a Turkish Delight. The plane jolted and angled up, the motors straining.

"What's going on!?" Came a call from Cindy, the cabin steward.

"We're aborting landing," Bill called into the mike. "Hold on."

Through the grey, dead ahead, Tucker knew Mt. Hood was looming up, directly in their flight path. Now that they were away and climbing again, he brought the flaps up and poured on the power, banking to port.

"Roger that."

Bill was talking to the tower and looked quickly at Tucker. "They've got a United coming down the gorge approach at four thousand, last contact. Something happened, it's off radar. Ground systems are down."

Tucker righted the plane but continued to climb. He felt sure that Mt. Hood would be safely off of starboard now. Altimeter read thirty nine. Need five hundred feet now! He pulled back on the yoke and gave full throttle. In seconds they broke out of the cloud cover, the sun momentarily blinding on the white clouds. Mt. Hood, huge and beautiful to starboard. Safely to starboard.

"Can you get a visual on the United?" he asked, continuing to climb and scanning the sky around them.

"No," Bill replied. "No, not....Yes, there, eleven o'clock." They saw the tail of the big 747 between the clouds to the west.

"Well, that was different," Tucker sighed. He eased the yoke forward and the jet leveled off, cruising east north east at seven thousand. Mt. Adams poked up through the clouds off the port side.

Bill gazed at him silently for a moment and raised his eyebrows. He picked up the cabin mike. "Ladies and gentlemen, we're above Portland. There is no danger to ship or passengers, but we had some problems on our approach due to weather and will be holding until we have clearance from the tower to land. There's a beautiful view of Mt. Hood for those on the right side of the plane. For those on the left, Mt. Adams is coming into view. The seatbelt sign is off in the event you would like to avail yourself of the facilities. Cabin crew, please check for shifted luggage. Thank you all for your patience." He clicked off and looked over to Tucker, who smiled at him.

"Avail yourself of the facilities. I like that, Bill. It sounds so much better than, "All of you who just shat yourselves might want to clean up.""

VII
Mountain View, California
NOAA- Global Atmospheric Monitoring Station

"Hey, give credit where credit is due. You're the one who picked up the anomaly on GAS 017." Dan smiled at Nancy from his monitor station. "The last twenty-four hours have been very intense," he added.

Nancy Stein shook her head wonderingly. "So they picked up the guy on the container ship and everybody else was dead? Take a day off and the world goes to hell." Dan shook a Pringles chip out of the can and munched down. "None of this is on the news, you know," she added.

Dan shrugged. "They haven't got a response yet. The Coast Guard has put out a quarantine warning and most of the traffic through there has been diverted. I heard from Casey over at NOAA that they've got the Navy in on the other rescues. The Canadians are helping too." He fished out another chip and examined it.

"The four other ships that aren't responding," Nancy said. "Where are they exactly?"

"All of them are well into the exclusion zone. The *Korean* is up on the northeast limit. They're trying to get the rescue helicopters out there but the electronics are all screwed up. The other three are pretty close to the middle."

Nancy looked at the gas data on her monitor, her brow furrowed. "I'm just trying to get up to speed here, Dan. What is the CDC saying?"

Dan put the examined chip into his mouth and munched

thoughtfully. He was enjoying Nancy having to come to him for the updates.

Nancy sat waiting for him to answer, thinking what a jerk he was.

"They've got samples from the gyre in the labs. The word so far is that it's some kind of marine fungal organism that's making the carbon monoxide. Another thing Casey said was a few of the lab guys think it's something new that got cooked up from all the tsunami garbage. But nobody really knows. The good news is that Boogie doesn't seem to be a human pathogen."

"Boogie?" Nancy blinked.

"Yeah. That's what they're calling it over at NOAA."

Dan held both hands aloft and wiggled his fingers. "As in Boogieman." His attempt at a scary face was merely stupid looking.

Nancy turned back to her monitor. "You and Ed deserve credit for calling it in, Dan. Getting the boat traffic diverted probably saved a lot of lives."

Dan felt surprise at her praise.

"Uh, yeah. I guess. Thanks."

July 20th

"Congratulations Kyle," Julie smiled, "One small step for man..."

Kyle laughed at her Apollo reference. Today was the anniversary of the first human landing on the moon, something she knew Kyle revered.

It was a bitter sweet reverence. She knew that too. One of her first serious conversations with him, that wasn't work related, had revealed the depth of his passion and frustration.

"You wanted to be an astronaut?"

It had surprised her, but then she thought, why not. He was bright and fit, the "right stuff". Of that she was certain. They sipped red wine, gazing out at the Golden Gate. Across the Bay, the lights were coming on in San Francisco.

Kyle had been bashful with her. This wasn't exactly a date. Just a couple of colleagues having a bit of supper and wine after work. But her question cracked something open, maybe with a little help from the wine.

"It wasn't just a kid's dream, like being a fireman or a cowboy or something." He gazed at her earnestly and something deep in his eyes took her breath away. All she could do was listen. "Every time an Apollo mission lifted off, that incredible Saturn Five, I felt like what was best about humanity was right there,

73

laid out for the whole world to see. We are explorers. Our destiny is out there."

She felt moved by the moisture in his eyes. It could have been corny, somebody getting misty about human space exploration. But when Kyle spoke she felt she could see out into the future too.

"All our eggs in this one precious basket, this Earth. We are life," he'd smiled, "maybe the only life in the neighborhood. We need to go back to the moon to stay, set up a permanent human presence. We'll learn what we need to know there in order to keep on going."

It had been an important conversation for them both. In her heart, Julie knew that was the moment she fell in love with him.

Now, she stood beside Kyle in the lab, several tanks bubbling on the counter. He responded to her "one small step" comment. "Thanks, Julie. Right now, it seems obvious. Your comment, about how a fungal mycelium spreads through bread really helped a lot."

"How so?" She was pleased by the compliment, but didn't see the connection.

"Well, remember how we talked about a mycelium needing a substrate? You know, something to invest and digest? And under the scope it appeared to be a mycelium structure attached to the spore matrix?"

She nodded and he went on. "I started thinking about the gyre, how the water itself is loaded with microfine plastic particles. I mean, most people hear there's this vast area of plastic garbage out in the Pacific and they imagine plastic bottles and cups and bags, like the beach after a busy weekend. That's out there, of course, but the real bulk is the fine stuff."

Julie met his gaze, following his logic. "That's it! That's why Boogie here wasn't producing any metabolites. The sea water in the tank had the normal fauna and flora but none of it was Boogie chow."

Julie paused to examine the sensors on the tank nearest her. The organism was now clearly emitting carbon monoxide. She peered in at the water.

"The water still looks clear. What substrate are you using?"

"Microbeads. Polyethylene microbeads," Kyle replied. "Tom had a bag full, down the hall in lab supplies. It's what they use in a lot of face washes as an abrasive."

Julie made a face. "So you, what, put in a couple of teaspoons and watched what happened?"

The mild challenge to his method in her eyes made him smile. "Not exactly. We did a series of serial dilutions and placed isolated samples of Boogie in each one, on monitors."

"And?"

"And any concentration over three hundred parts per million yielded biological activity."

Julie took in the info and nodded.

"Therefore Boogie eats plastic and gives off carbon monoxide as a metabolic byproduct. It's got to have pretty sharp teeth to break a stable carbon to carbon bond." Kyle's eyes twinkled. He loved the discovery game and Julie was a competent partner. "Well consider your *Rhizobium*. The triple bond in atmospheric nitrogen is a pretty tough nut. Other than a lightning strike it's only your bacterial friends who've figured it out."

Julie grinned at that. "So you're probably looking for an enzyme-coenzyme system. *Rhizobium* has a nitrogenase based on molybdenum and iron. If I was going to make a carbonase I imagine I'd look to the metalo-enzymes first."

"Good line of inquiry," Kyle responded. "What we saw in Samuelson's lab was a remarkable metabolic versatility in fungi. There was significant gene duplication and horizontal gene transfer. And that interacted with clustered and non-clustered metabolic pathways."

Julie took it in. "An accelerated metabolic evolution that would be strongly environmental dependent. But not a candidate for a marine family tree, you thought."

Kyle looked into the tank. "I remember something from undergrad ecology that struck me as very true. We were talking about niches, how organisms and their environments shaped each other. We were doing a field study, camped out in the desert on the east side of the San Gabriels in SoCal. It seemed to me that there were a lot of opportunities, food supplies out in the desert that nobody was using. All available niches weren't being exploited. Doc Bartholomew said this is a snapshot of right now. Ecological forces express themselves through time so you have to think through time to appreciate them. No large food supply will go forever untapped in an evolving system. Some organism will arise in time that can utilize that substrate." Kyle looked sideways at Julie. "I think that's what we're looking at here. The plastic concentration in the gyre constitutes an untapped food supply." He tapped the tank. "Boogie here has figured out how to utilize that food supply."

Julie shrugged. "Then Boogie may ultimately be a good thing, breaking down all the plastics and elastomers and fibers we're flooding the world with. Real biodegradation of the pollution."

"There's that," Kyle agreed. "If we can control it. The problem, as I see it, isn't the carbon monoxide metabolite. Cars put out carbon monoxide and we work with it. No, the problem is the mechanism of spore dispersal. It won't stay in the gyre. The winds will take it everywhere."

Kyle stood by silently while the substance of what he'd said sunk in.

Julie's eyes widened when she got it.

"Oh my god," she said quietly, "What doesn't have plastic in it these days?"

II
Lincoln City, Oregon Coast
Plastic World

Ben was surprised and more than a bit annoyed when he turned into the parking space in front of the store. The neon Open sign was still lit up in the front window. Inside, the overhead lights were on too. He'd left Phil to lock up yesterday afternoon and gone home to watch the Mariners game.

"Better be a darned good reason," he thought. "Maybe he came in early and opened."

Ben pushed at the front glass door and it swung open.

"He must be here. Why would he come in early?"

Ben moved into the store. What was that smell? Like a motor oil.

He surveyed the showroom. It seemed so dingy all of a sudden. The sound of a radio at the rear sales desk.

"Phil?" he called out. "Phil, what are you doing in already?"

He made his way down the aisle of storage bins towards the back. The bins were discolored, a black oily sheen on their surfaces.

"What the hell is this?"

He was about to run a finger down the nearest bin when he spotted Phil, asleep at the desk. He was dead out, sprawled across the paper work that littered the desktop.

"Phil! Hey, what's going on? Are you drunk? Come on, wake...."

He stopped.

Phil's eyes were wide open, unseeing. The skin of his face was flushed, lips an odd cherry red.

"Phil, oh my God."

He put a hand on the boy's forehead. Cold.

Ben's hand was shaking as he dialed 911. He couldn't look away from the surprised, innocent face.

"Operator, Yes. There's an emergency. I don't know. Maybe a heart attack. I think the boy is dead."

He answered a few more questions, but began to feel like he weighed a thousand pounds. Ben leaned on the desk. The telephone receiver, moist and greasy, slipped from his hand and clattered to the tiles.

He slumped to his knees and was only slightly aware of the rubber thud when his face hit the floor.

III
Crescent City, California

The customer stream at EZ-Wash was lower today. People were reluctant to get their car washed if they thought it was going to get rained on and road slopped the moment they pulled out into the street. But rain wasn't in the forecast. The low cloud cover, a fog really, was normal for this time of year. Maybe just not a carwash day.

For the millionth time, Roberto Sanchez let his mind deliver up memories of his warm Nayarit. Mexico had its share of problems, that was for certain. But at least, he thought, you didn't freeze your ass off twenty-four hours a day.

"Hey, Guapo! Tienes cigarro?"

He looked over at Luis and nodded.

Luis tucked his rag in a back pocket and strolled over to where Roberto was leaning against the building. There was a car coming through the auto wash section, but they still had a couple of minutes.

With the rag hanging down his thin backside, Roberto thought Luis looked like a squirrel. He pulled the box of Marlboros out of his shirt pocket.

"Tienes cerillos, Flaco? Acabo!"

He shook his empty matchbox and Luis smiled.

"Mejor que cerillos, cabron."

Luis produced an antique Zippo lighter. Both men smoked silently. The roar of the wind tunnel dryer made conversation too much effort.

The big Dodge SUV emerged and Luis stubbed out his smoke, saving the butt for later. He went around to the driver's side and pulled the vehicle down to the vacuum and hand finishing area. Roberto joined him and they set to work with the speed and efficiency that comes from practice.

A hefty gringo in a plaid Pendleton walked out of the coffee shed holding a large, steaming paper cup. He made his way over and watched the two men work. Roberto had seen him around, drinking beer at the 101 Club with his trucker buddies.

"Hello" Roberto smiled.

The man, middle aged, a bit overweight and in need of a shave acknowledged him. Not unfriendly, but no recognition. They'd shot a game of Eight Ball last month, but if he remembered Roberto it didn't show in his grey eyes.

Roberto raised up the rear door to begin the interior wipe down. It was a new car and the carpeted deck was spotless. The plastic sides, however, were smudged and oily. He used the hand sprayer to lay down a mist of the interior cleaner and grabbed a couple more rags. To his surprise the first pass did not leave a newly cleaned surface. Instead the black smudge remained, now resolved into stripes. A few bits of white lint from the terry cloth clung to the panel. He gave it another spray and wiped again. Now a significant amount of the black came away with the cloth, but the panel color was wrong, the textured grain of the plastic deformed. It was like spreading frosting on one of Abuela's cakes.

"What the fuck are you doing, boy?"

Roberto turned to see the glaring face of the gringo peering into the rear compartment.

He reached in and rubbed his finger down a panel. It left a long smudge in the softened plastic.

The man grabbed the unmarked spray bottle away from Roberto.

"God Damn it! This is a new car."

He examined the bottle then shook it in Roberto's face.

"What is this shit?"

The face of the manager, Miguel, had appeared at the office window when the shouting started. He now made haste to engage the gringo.

"Mr. Perkins, hello. What's the problem, sir?"

"The problem," bellowed Mr. Perkins, "is that this stupid wetback used paint remover or something. Look for yourself."

Miguel's smile of appeasement faded when he looked into the rear of the SUV. He turned on Roberto and demanded in English, "What cleaner did you use?"

Roberto, surprised and defensive, pointed to the bottle that Mr. Perkins now held. "Regular one," he managed.

Miguel held out his hand to Mr. Perkins. "May I?" he asked.

He squeezed a few sprays into his hand. The light, perfumed detergent water dripped off his fingers. He smelled it and rubbed his hand. "I don't understand, Mr. Perkins. This isn't anything out of the ordinary, just some mild detergent." Miguel nodded toward the smudged interior, "It wouldn't do this."

"Well God Damn it, it did do it. And you are responsible. I'm not taking this bullshit."

Mr. Perkins pulled out his cell phone and began to dial. Then he stopped and looked at his hand.

"What the.."

An oily black syrup coated his palm. The phone case seemed to be melting.

IV
Mountain View, California
NOAA- Global Atmospheric Monitoring Station

"You're kidding? Them too? God Casey, thanks for keeping us in the loop. This is nuts. Yeah, OK. Talk to you later."

Dan put his Smartphone down on the desk and, for once, sat in stunned silence.

Nancy and Ed stood nearby. Ed prompted, "So?"

Dan shook his head. "This is getting very weird. Now Homeland Security is involved. There are reports of electrical malfunctions coming in from all along the northern coast. Even deaths. Casey said a kid died in a store up in Lincoln City, on the Oregon coast. The owner called 911 then passed out himself. Carbon monoxide poisoning. He said the team NOAA flew up there is seeing the same thing they did in Portland, when navigation went down yesterday."

Nancy asked, "You mean the insulation melting off the wires?"

Dan nodded, looking distracted. "Yeah, yeah. Insulation, tires on cars, cellphone towers going down. Homeland Security is talking bioterrorism, like we were under attack. They're co-opting everybody. Now it's their show."

"Jesus," Ed whistled. "How did we get here?"

V
Oakland, California
Citigen

"Can they really do that to us, Dave?"

Kyle and Julie stood with two dozen others in the big conference room at Citigen.

"Yes, Paul, they can. Homeland Security has upgraded this to a possible terrorist attack. They are calling the shots."

Dave Davenport looked harried. He waved over to Kyle. "Dr. Hoffman, can you share with all present what you've told me. And," he looked meaningfully around the room, "this is confidential and not for public consumption. NOAA is working up a statement for this afternoon. This is breaking open whether they want it to or not. There's too much coming out of the Northwest right now, and the news outlets are connecting dots and asking questions. OK, go ahead Kyle."

It was mostly a young to early middle age campus and Kyle felt comfortable addressing the group as an equal. He nodded acknowledgement to Dave and began.

"Afternoon. Well, as you're all aware, we've been working with the samples of Boogie that NOAA brought us on Wednesday. What we know so far is that the organism is likely a fungi in the *Ascomycetes* class. It doesn't match anything in the database exactly, but is close to terrestrial forms. Carbon monoxide is one of its metabolic products and the nutritional substrate seems to be any kind of plastic. We have activity with polyethylenes, polypropylenes and polystyrenes. The preliminary results for elastomers and fibers are also positive." Kyle nodded to Julie. "Dr. Newsom and I have traced the carbonase activity. Following her lead, we have isolated a pair of enzymes. One of them, built around arsenic and iron, appears to be responsible for Boogie's ability to break the carbon to carbon bond in artificial polymers. Dr. Newsom?"

Julie smiled at him.

"The pathway leading to carbon monoxide appears to be a parallel to fermentation, but less efficient in ATP production. We have found an additional metabolite of molecular hydrogen that was not noted until we had the closed systems, probably due to low density dissipation."

Kyle walked over to the big white board and picked up a black marker. "So here's what we've got." He proceeded to draw a mass that looked like spaghetti. Sprouting off the spaghetti he drew vertical tubes that ended in "string of pearls" looking structures.

"The spore dispersal mechanism is what we'd see in a terrestrial fungi. Apparently the so called smog pilots on the rescue missions describe is an airborne spore dispersal. Reports along the northwest coast of disruption to the plastic infrastructure support the contention that Boogie spores are blowing in and are responsible."

"Kyle?" Tom Whitcombe raised a hand like he was in school.

"Tom?" Kyle said.

"Homeland is suggesting this is a bioterror attack. It does seem to have come out of nowhere. Can you comment?"

"Thanks, Tom. Yes, it does seem to have come out of nowhere. Let me bore you for a minute more. Here's a working hypothesis." Kyle used a green marker to write the word *Mycelium* with an arrow pointing to the spaghetti. He scribbled a bit in the mass with the green to make it clear which part he was labeling. Then, with a red marker he wrote *Conidia* and *Spores* and added some color to the vertical tubes and string of pearls.

"We think Boogie is something new - a marine adapted terrestrial form. I know that Dr. Logan suggested detritus from the Japanese tsunami may have been the seed stock and that is perfectly possible. The thing about fungi is that they can go along quite merrily as just a mycelium, growing and developing almost invisibly. Think about mushrooms, how they seem to just pop up after a rain. They are the fruiting body of a pre-existing mycelium in the soil. They aren't like a radish or some plant that grows from a seed, more like how a plum forms on an existing plum tree in the spring. When conditions are right, the mycelium rapidly develops the spore producing body. One minute there's nothing there, next day the lawn is covered in toadstools."

Kyle looked around the room. A few heads were nodding with understanding.

"I'd suggest that Boogie has been with us for quite a while, but under the radar, small patches of bloom not producing enough carbon monoxide to get our attention. We don't know what the timing is on the life cycle yet. It is likely that the massive bloom we're seeing is the result of previous blooms and significant spore dispersal around the eastern gyre. The now established mycelium, eating the microplastics suddenly blooms. Where there was no apparent organism, suddenly the surface of the sea is coated with a spore producing mat."

"You're suggesting," Tom said, "that this is a natural phenomenon and not, as Homeland Security asserts, a possible bioterror attack?"

Kyle wanted to speak carefully and precisely. He didn't really believe this conversation was going to remain confidential.

"Tom, I'd say it's an act of war, the same way a bacterial infection is an act of war. At this point we have no evidence that Boogie is a human created organism. What I think we can say is that the spore cloud will spread, further fungal infections will occur, and that will lead to further spore production. The northwest infections demonstrate that Boogie will not be constrained to a marine environment. As far as I can tell Boogie is an equal opportunity plastic eater. We are very much at risk. Homeland Security has it right at that level. But I don't think that some group of bad guys has set the Boogieman on us." Kyle hesitated and pulled out a line from the movie, Jurassic Park. "Life finds a way. Boogie was inevitable because there is a vast, ready food supply in the form of artificial polymers. Is it a GMO monster set upon us by our enemies? That's for better minds than mine to decide. My job, our job, is to use what we know to give Boogie a fatal nosebleed."

Julie took her cue.

"In our lab, we've used a Trojan Horse to introduce a *Rhizobium* genome into the nodule formation process to create self-inoculating nitrogen fixation. What Kyle, Dr. Hoffman, and I propose is to introduce, via horizontal gene transfer, a Trojan Horse into Boogie's genome to deactivate its carbonase activity. Give it a cold so it starves to death."

As that bit sank into the assembly, Dave Davenport moved to the center.

"Homeland Security has requested the resources of Citigen to find a response to this threat. And make no mistake. It is a serious and imminent threat to our entire infrastructure. We don't have the luxury of time on this one. You are the brightest group of people I know. I want proposals, either cooperation or new avenues of exploration. We need to contain this before we end up back in the Stone Age, sitting in the fungal rotted remains of our technological society. Let's get to work."

On the way back down to their lab, Kyle and Julie reflected on the meeting.

"Do you think Dave was overly dramatic there at the end?" she smiled.

Kyle laughed.

"Overly dramatic? Well, it was unexpected coming from him, I admit. And yet he might not be too far wrong. Remember the hurricane in New Orleans? Take out the electrical grid, communications, transportation and all hell breaks loose. I've heard it said that if the world falls too far back down the ladder of development it can be nearly impossible to climb back up. If I imagine a world without electricity it's a very different level of civilization. I could get by without plastic bags and garbage cans, but without insulation on wires the whole thing comes crashing down."

Julie was thoughtful as they walked. "If we're going to be stuck with Boogie, maybe we can come up with resistant polymers for insulation?"

Kyle nodded in agreement. "That'll probably be necessary no matter what. Boogie is one genie that's going to be hard to put back into the bottle. What scares me is the disruption of services in between. Everything is going to rot to a halt. I think it will be a very grim time ahead if we don't succeed here in stopping it, and fast."

On that sobering note, they arrived at their clean, well-lit lab.

VI
West Marin, California
WRAP offices

The Wilderness Renewal and Protection offices were located not far from Lagunitas, in the canyon after leaving Samuel Taylor Park. The cabin was purloined from the original owners by the Park Service and should have been demolished, in keeping with the charter. Luckily Chuck Coker, the head of the Environmental Warriors organization in New York City, had taken a personal interest in WRAP, providing both legal and financial support. He had leaned on the Park Service to back off on the demolition and hand the property over to WRAP, presented now as a "non-profit educational foundation with broad public support."

Hank sat outside near the fire pit enjoying the aroma of warm Bay Laurel and the gentle gurgle of Lagunitas Creek. The sound of a screen door banging shut and a crunch of shoes on gravel announced Joan arriving with a late lunch. She only worked half days on Fridays and had come home early so they could enjoy this time together.

"Barbequed tofu, avocado and sprouts on ciabatta," she announced.

Hank smiled down at the sandwiches. It was an understood by the staff at WRAP that vegetarian, preferably vegan, wasn't just a good, healthy choice. It was the right moral and ethical choice. For his part, Hank preferred a good Reuben at the brew pub. He loved Joan though, and appreciated her effort on the sandwiches. And they were delicious, no doubt about that.

"Great," he said while chewing. The Pale Ale went well with

the mild spice of the tofu. One concession at WRAP was Lagunitas Pale Ale. The refrigerator in the cabin kitchen had a good supply of the local brew, and on Fridays it was understood that "chill-out time" started at four o'clock.

Technically Hank was about two and a half hours ahead of schedule, but nobody minded. It had been a good week for WRAP. A lawsuit they had filed almost three years ago, to compel residents along the creek watershed to remove non-native yard plantings, had been decided in their favor. If it wasn't part of the original flora of the watershed, it would have to go. The WRAP master plan called for the removal of all human influence within a hundred meters of the creek to "restore the native salmon run and protect the endangered population."

Hank shook his head, remembering the ugly anger in the faces of the creek residents at the last county meeting. They just couldn't grasp the importance of restoring the creek so that the Coho salmon run might one day be vibrant and sustainable again. This really was the last stand for the wild Coho in Marin County. All the old timers who had their homes along the creek were an impediment, but Environmental Warriors had deep pockets and lots of donors. They'd get them out eventually.

"So I guess congratulations are in order," Joan smiled. She lifted her bottle of beer and they clinked a toast.

"To all of us environmental warriors. May we prevail." Hank grinned. "The job now is to get compliance. That's going to be the rough part. I ran into Mrs. Pollak at the Post Office. She started screaming at me about her rose garden, how her grandmother had those roses brought out from back east in nineteen-oh-one."

Joan shook her head. "The old guard will go out screaming. Their generation thinks that property rights outweigh animal rights. You'll never convince them otherwise."

Hank nodded. "You got that right. She said if any WRAP workers show up on her property and try to tear out her garden, she'll shoot them."

"You're kidding! Oh Hank, you've got to let the sheriff know what she said. She'd kill somebody over her rosebushes. What's the matter with people?" Joan shook her head in wonder.

"People hate change," Hank intoned, "but change is coming. Like the birth of a baby, there has to be some pain when you bring something new into the world."

He smiled to himself, thinking about Mr. Lynas and Citigen. Tomorrow afternoon, Larry would come by the house and Mr. Lynas would be on his way.

"Sometimes you have to break a few eggs to make an omelette," he said.

Joan nodded.

"You got that right."

VII
Seattle
Department of Homeland Security Press Room

"Good afternoon, members of the Press. I realize it's late and we've got a lot to cover, so if you'll take your seats we can get going."

Paula Dinesh felt like the sacrificial lamb. Her hastily compiled notes did not have the level of organization or clarity deemed professional. But Nick had been called to the emergency NOAA meeting and so the press conference fell to her as assistant bureau chief. The hubbub in the room quieted and a few dozen faces sat gazing at her expectantly.

"Let's begin with what we know," she said.

"Is the United States under attack? No evasions. Just answer the question!" Paula gazed coldly at the Fox reporter. If she lost control right now, this would be a disaster. She ignored him.

"Two days ago the US Coast Guard received an emergency distress call from a container vessel approximately six hundred miles off the Washington coast. At the same time a NOAA monitoring station picked up a very large cell of carbon monoxide gas in the same region."

"I'll ask again," the Fox News reporter stood and shouted, "Are we under attack?"

"Sit down and shut up, Leo. Let the woman speak."

Leo glared at the other reporter but reluctantly seated himself.

"We regret to report that the Coast Guard rescue team

found only one crewman alive. He is recovering and plans are underway to recover the vessel when it emerges from the toxic zone. At this point the ship is proceeding eastward on the autopilot, and we anticipate a crew will board and bring it under control by noon tomorrow. The toxic zone has been quarantined, but there remain four other vessels within that are not responding."

Paula pulled out the next note card and proceeded. "The cause of the toxic gas is apparently biological, and NOAA has identified the source as a marine fungal bloom, similar to a red tide. At this point," she looked at Leo critically, "we have no indication that this is anything other than a natural phenomenon but on a vast scale. That said, the DHS has mobilized an emergency response due to the continuing and growing disruptions to the technological infrastructure along the West Coast of the United States. We are seeing outages on the electrical grid and telecommunications, especially as related to cell towers. The scientific consensus is that the airborne spores of this organism, carried ashore by winds, are responsible.

"The CDC has assured us that, at this point, the spores do not appear to pose a disease threat to humans or animals. Work is progressing to characterize the organism and updates will be given as they become available."

Paula restacked her cards and looked out at the group. "So, questions? Yes, Allan."

"Paula, our affiliate in Portland reports that the navigational array at Portland International went down yesterday and they've been unable to restore it to service. Is this related to the fungal spore infestation and what is DHS doing to protect vulnerable installations and public safety?"

Paula opened a small binder and extracted a paper. "Thanks Allan, this is the preliminary on the Portland array. The NOAA investigators report the insulation on the electronics had been compromised by fungal infection. Backups are being installed and disinfected. We expect to see service restored by tomorrow morning. The DHS has a catalogue of vulnerable installations and teams are doing a triage to keep essential services in operation."

"Paula, how are they disinfecting electronics?"

The questioner, a tall woman from the local PBS station, was known to Paula as the science editor. They'd met during her presentation on global warming organized at Paula's son's school in the Spring.

"Hi Judy. That's probably something you'd know more about than me. My understanding is that this organism isn't some kind of superbug. It cleans up like any sort of mildew, with a mild beach or peroxide solution. The NOAA and our people are installing high output ultraviolet lights in the critical circuit boxes, where a liquid disinfectant wouldn't be practical. A longer horizon response is being formulated, and I can't give any more detail than that."

A hand waved at the rear.

"Melanie?"

"Thanks. We're hearing reports of several deaths down on the coast that seem to be related. A carbon monoxide poisoning in Lincoln City. One of our correspondents reported a plastics store where the contents were decomposing. They used the word melting."

Paula swallowed and nodded. "I know that NOAA had some of the Portland team down there today, but I haven't seen the report yet. This is developing quickly and when we have more information it will be made available."

"Paula!" "Paula!"

Paula looked out over the assembly of waving hands seeking her attention.

"You owe me big for this one, Nick," she thought to herself.

She peered at the name tag on the man in the front row who was smiling at her and raising just one finger. "Mr. Morley, yes?"

"Steve Morley, Seattle Sun. Paula, this thing you keep referring to as *the organism*. Friends in the Coast Guard tell me it has a working name of Boogie. Is there any evidence that Boogie is a GMO? Something out of a lab?"

The room went very quiet.

"Mr. Morley, as was stated at the beginning of this interview, at this time Boogie or whatever you want to call it is being viewed as a purely natural phenomenon. There is no evidence, none whatsoever, to suggest anything different."

Morley shrugged and said, "It's odd though, don't you think, that we've never seen or heard of anything like this before. I mean, we've heard of flesh eating bacteria and avian flu and incurable tuberculosis. But a bug that eats plastic, which is what you're saying even if you're not saying it, that's something brand new. I'm hearing suggestions that it's some ecological experiment to clean up plastic garbage that got away from the GMO cowboys. Any comment?"

Morley had a sly smile.

Paula suddenly disliked him very much.

VIII
Fort Bragg, California
Early evening

Living right on the coast had advantages and disadvantages. The salt mist swirled up from the crashing waves, worked its way into the air and crept inland. All that iodine made for fewer goiters. But if you were made out of iron it was a decided liability.

Trevor wiggled the key in the ignition of his vintage jeep again. The corrosion had taken a toll on the old girl, but he wasn't one to give up on a friend.

"Come on, Gina. You can do it."

There was no sign of life. He pulled on the headlights and had to admit the battery was likely dead again. It was too new to be sulfated. He had a creeping suspicion that the gradual loss was due to some grounding problem. It made his heart sink to think about all the time that tracing it would require.

Trevor stepped out, closed the car door and walked the twenty feet to Tom Hutchen's front porch. The duplex had this shared carport and it made it convenient for a guy to ask a neighbor for a jump. He didn't want to wear it out by asking too many times, though.

"Hey Tom," Trevor greeted the older man.

Tom was absorbed at his work table, the hanging light reflecting off his bald head. A partially disassembled laptop did not look happy. When Tom looked up his face was a mask of irritation.

"Huh? Oh, hello Trev."

He refocused down on the computer. The back was off and a can of WD40 sat beside a crumpled pile of paper towels.

"I think the damn battery leaked. Look at this mess!" He motioned toward the black stained paper towels on the table. Trevor leaned over and looked down.

"The big six-volt battery in my lantern did that last summer," he clucked sympathetically.

"At least it didn't blow up like some of those lithium batteries are doing."

Tom shook his head.

"Well, thank God for small favors."

He sprayed a shot of the WD 40 into the battery well of the computer and daubed at it with a fresh paper towel. Suddenly he looked up at Trevor, as if realizing for the first time he had company.

"Trevor! Sorry, what can I do for you?"

"I have to bother you again for a jump on Gina. She's not holding the charge."

Tom shook his head ruefully. "Electronics! What would we do without them. I'm not getting anywhere with this mess. Let's go give Gina a goose." He stood and wiped his hands. "I'll get my keys. Meet you out there."

Trevor nodded and made his way down the porch steps and over to the carport. He opened the rear door behind the driver's seat and tugged out his jumper cables and emergency lantern. When he fingered the button, the light flooded the now darkened carport. "At least this works," he thought.

Reaching in under the dash, he popped the hood release.

Tom came out of the house and slipped behind the wheel of his Explorer.

"God Damn it!" Trevor heard from within the vehicle.

"What's up?" he asked tentatively.

"I'd say we're both up shit creek, Trev. My battery is dead too."

He heard the click and clunk of Tom pulling his own hood release and came around to meet him with the light. Tom searched along the inner edge of the hood and popped the safety latch. They both looked into the Explorer engine compartment. Trevor didn't understand what he was seeing. Tom was too stunned to speak.

The light reflected off a dozen small black pools dotting the engine block. The big hose to the radiator draped limply down, absurdly shortened. A few drops of the green coolant oozed slowly down the back of the grill. The now bare wires coming off the battery were oily black, the lingering odor of burned rubber where the line had shorted against the block.

"What is going on here?" Tom asked, his voice leaden and flat.

As if on cue, the lights in his house winked out. The two men stood together in the carport, illuminated by Trevor's lantern.

"No idea," Trevor replied.

They both stepped out under the overcast sky. In both directions along the coast, normally twinkling with lights at the coming of night, there was only darkness.

July 21st

"Morning Dr. Hoffman. Working the weekend too?"

Kyle smiled an acknowledgement. "Morning Neal, morning Mike. Yeah, we've got an experiment in progress that takes some babysitting. Is Dr. Newsom in yet?"

Neal Brody nodded. He was a big man, a linebacker type. The clipboard in his huge hand looked almost like a three by five card. "Yes, she came in about half an hour ago with Dr. Whitcombe."

Kyle took that in, then asked, "Is Dave Davenport here?"

"Yup. And quite a few others," Neal said. Concern showed on his meaty face.

Kyle turned and began to walk away from the security building.

"Dr. Hoffman?"

Kyle stopped and met the eyes of Mike Penn, the other security guard. Mike had a cherubic face, but Kyle knew his Mixed Martial Arts credentials and respected the strength of the man.

"Yes, Mike?"

"Well sir, last night we watched the news and they talked about this Boogie infection that's hitting the northwest. I understand that you can't talk about what's going on in there," he nodded towards the Citigen building, "but my wife's a nurse, as you know. She asked me to ask you if you had any advice for us." He held Kyle with his ice blue eyes, his face an open appeal for the truth.

Kyle shifted uncomfortably. "I saw the report on the PBS Newshour," Kyle began, "and I believe the CDC is correct. It's not a plague or disease humans can catch, as far as anyone knows. What they suggested is good. There may be some disruption in services like electrical supply or cell networks. I think we'd all be smart to go over our earthquake emergency supplies and be certain to have a few days of food and water, just in case."

He saw the disappointment in the man's eyes, his acceptance that the power structure is never going to give it to you straight.

"If I were you, I'd make sure my emergency water was in glass bottles," Kyle added.

Mike nodded, glad for the bone, not demanding more.

The two men watched Kyle's back as he headed up the walkway towards the main lab building.

"Do you believe him?" Neal asked.

"I think he's a good guy. He told us as much as he's allowed I suppose," Mike replied.

"I listened to KSFO coming in this morning. The Lame Stream media isn't talking about it, but they think this Boogie thing came out of a lab somewhere."

Mike tried to avoid political discussions with Neal. He liked him well enough. Sometimes they'd have a beer together after a shift, if it wasn't the midnight to eight haul. But Neal liked all the conspiracy theory crap and it just wasn't worth going down that road yet again.

"Yeah, I don't know."

This was going to be a long double shift. If he was going to be here until midnight even double pay would not compensate for having to listen to Neal channeling KSFO. Change the subject.

"Dr. Newsom looked great this morning, didn't she?"

Mike knew Neal would rather talk about beautiful women than conspiracy theories. It was his default re-direction in conversations with Neal. And of course, Neal wasn't fooled. Over the last few years it had evolved into a respectful signal that said, "Let's not go there." It was their idiosyncratic version of, "How about those Niners?"

"Oh boy, did she ever," Neal agreed.

"It's funny calling somebody that cute Doctor."

II
Citigen

"Morning Julie." Kyle put his case down on the lab counter and extracted his laptop. "How are we doing?"

Dr. Julie Newsom looked over at Kyle, the pupils in her eyes huge. Kyle felt the breath catch in his throat. There were moments lately when all he wanted from life was to fall into the well of those eyes.

"I think we're moving very much in the right direction, Dr. Hoffman," she grinned, and Kyle returned to earth. "I think using the Cpf1 is our way in. I sent you the file this morning."

Kyle opened the encrypted message and scanned the data. "This is good. I'm taking this to the meeting. Shall we go?"

They linked arms as they walked down the hall, Kyle whistling "We're off to see the Wizard".

Dave Davenport looked less happy than usual. He prowled the front of the little conference room. Seated to his right was a tidy little man that Kyle did not recognize. He leaned over to Julie. "Who's that?" he whispered.

"I think it's the FEMA guy," she whispered back. The smell of her hair was enchanting. She could whisper in his ear all day.

"Let's get started," Dave said authoritatively.

"I want to introduce Dr. Richard Glass. Dr. Glass comes to us from FEMA. As we have previously discussed, this is a confidential briefing. What is said here stays here. Dr. Glass?"

"Thanks Dave. I'll cut to the chase. FEMA is a department of DHS. We are involved because of what appears to be a looming natural disaster. In less than sixty hours a high pressure front moving down out of the Gulf of Alaska will sweep across the northeastern Pacific and push the spore cloud over most of the western United States. What has been a trickle of incidents precipitated by the fungal organism will likely become a flood."

Julie unconsciously took Kyle's hand and squeezed it.

"Our computer model suggests that within nine days of exposure the western electrical grid will have failed, along with telecom relays and most transportation links."

Dr. Glass surveyed the room. The assembly of scientists were stunned by the impact of what he'd just said.

"We are currently mobilizing emergency supplies and setting up staging centers, similar to the hurricane response centers you've all seen during the last big storms to hit the southeast. The challenge with this one is that we aren't talking about a storm that will pass.

"Citigen is involved because we have a very narrow window in which to act. Your proposal to introduce a genetic modification into the fungal mass to interfere with its metabolism is seen by many research associates at FEMA as the most effective course of action. That is if, and only if, there can be a high probability, a very high probability, that the modification will not migrate to other species.

"That's a tall order in the best of times, as everyone in this room is aware."

Dr. Glass leaned over to Dave and quietly asked something. Dave nodded and looked up, catching Julie's eye.

"Dr. Newsom, will you please describe to us the data you relayed to me this morning?"

Kyle felt Julie's nails dig into his palm. Then she stood. "We sequenced two enzymes from Boogie. One, an arsenic based metalo-enzyme responsible for the carbonase activity, the breaking of the bonds between the plastic molecules. The other, part of the oxidative phosphorylation pathway, the energy pathway for the organism. The data that Dave is speaking about is the identification of unique sequences on the fungal DNA where we can cut and insert our Trojan Horse. These staggered sequence pairs do not occur anywhere else in the world genomic database."

Dr. Glass inclined his head and smiled at her. "So your Trojan Horse will block the organism's ability to eat, but not affect any other living thing? Very elegant, Dr. Newsom. Can you give me a timeframe?"

Julie looked down at Kyle. The love and pride she saw in his eyes elicited an electrical frisson down her spine.

"Kyle, Dr. Hoffman, and our team will begin construction today. We have a good degree of confidence that we'll be able to synthesize the interrupter package and delivery system, based on previous work. If we are able to do so, we'll run the trial as soon as possible."

Dr. Glass steepled his fingers. "Wonderful work. All of you. I wish we had more time. It would be best if we had all this yesterday," he smiled. "I'll carry all of this back to DC this morning. If we can get an emergency EPA waiver based on analysis of your data, we might have a chance against this thing."

Dave stood up and spoke. "OK people. We're all on this now. I need to ask all of you to coordinate work schedules with Sally. We're going to be on this twenty-four-seven until we've got a solution."

III
Lagunitas, West Marin, California

"Joan? You seen my wallet? I thought I put it in the chest drawer here."

Hank stood before the heavy oak chest near the front door. The middle drawer was pulled open. He bent slightly, peering into the rat's nest of car keys and house keys and loose birthday candles and rubber bands. But no wallet.

"Check your shorts," Joan called from the bedroom.

Hank padded back into the den. The big wide couch where they had celebrated last night was still draped with his plaid shirt and shorts. In the morning Joan had discreetly collected her clothing and it was already deposited in the laundry.

He lifted the cargo shorts and knew immediately from the weight in the pocket that she was right. "Got it. Thank you."

Back in the kitchen, Hank depressed the button on the toaster oven again to give his bagel a little more of a toasting. Joan entered, dressed in a breezy summer dress, large red poppies on an off-white background.

"Don't you look nice," he smiled approvingly. "Where are you and your sister going?"

"Lou likes dim-sum so probably someplace near her house. Maybe Hong Kong East Pacific, in Emeryville. They've got a good view out towards the Bay Bridge."

"Crowded on a Saturday morning though," Hank raised his eyebrows in an "I told you so" expression.

"They've got a lot of tables. Be back around three. I'll call when I'm coming through San Rafael. Think about what you want for dinner and I'll pick it up."

They hugged and she moved towards the front door. "Hope you and your friend have a good hike," she called back brightly.

Hank walked into the living room and gazed out, watching her descend the steps down to the cars. It worked well that she was joining her sister for brunch. There'd be no importunate questions about the ice chest or Larry.

At that moment Larry Burnham was exiting the freeway into San Rafael. His mouth was dry, now that D-Day had arrived. In various guises, he'd taken part in quite a number of EarthFirst actions over the years, both in the USA and abroad. There was always the sense of being a guerilla, a David standing against Goliaths. Three years ago they had spiked a lot of old growth redwoods up in Humboldt. The lumber company had men with dogs and bright searchlights. Keeping ahead of them reminded him of those war movies where the escaped POWs were just a few steps ahead of the Nazis pursuing them. He was proud of the EarthFirst record. Even though the media labeled them terrorists, no person had ever been directly killed in any of their actions. There had been injuries when saw blades hit spikes, that was true. But no fatalities.

This action with Hank was taking it to a whole new level. It had been an idea more than a year ago for Larry to get hired on at Citigen. He was the sleeper, and the original plan was sabotage, similar to their action in the Central Valley two years back. By working on the inside they were able to torch the whole GMO soybean test plot farm.

His chance meeting with Hank Meyers at the rally last Autumn had opened the door on this larger, more dramatic action. This was not to be an EarthFirst operation. It needed to be very much on the QT. It's not every day you meet a fellow traveler with thirty pounds of C-4 and detonator expertise. Hank and he had put the plan together in sworn secrecy. It was their baby. Maybe someday they'd be considered heroes.

Larry turned left into Central San Rafael and headed west towards Lagunitas. It was only about twelve miles from the freeway, but a different world. West Marin was living proof that a few dedicated people can stop the machine of rapacious development.

Hank finished his bagel and coffee. Larry would be arriving soon and Hank wanted all the ducks in a row before he got here. If anybody looked in the ice chest they'd see Dr. Peppers and Cokes, some Subway sandwiches, the plastic bag of napkins and an ice bag. Just what you'd expect in the lunch box of the night shift janitor.

He trudged up the hill to the workshop. Mr. Lynas was good to go, except for attaching the timer circuit. Hank hefted the ice chest up onto his work bench and opened the lid. A neatly trimmed layer of Styrofoam concealed the blocks of C-4 taped to the floor of the case. He lifted the side, revealing a little cubby between the blocks of explosive where the cellphone timer was to fit. A pair of thin wires terminating in male banana plugs led to the detonator proper in the corner.

Hank had checked and double checked the cellphone to be certain no accidental incoming call could lead to a premature detonation. The phone clock read ten forty seven a.m. on Saturday, July 21st. The alarm was set for three a.m. on July 22nd.

"Here's your wake up call, Mr. Lynas," he thought grimly.

With great delicacy and wearing disposable gloves, Hank inserted the banana pins into the sockets emerging from the cellphone housing and adjusted the waterproof sleeve around the unit. A final sealing with silicon and placement.

"The key," Larry had counseled, "is no forensic evidence. Nothing linking you and Mr. Lynas. Nothing at all, including me."

The very last step would be to arm the detonator, and Larry would do that when Mr. Lynas was in position.

Hank was no fool. This device lifted him out of the Eco-vandal club. The bomb and the bomber would be considered a terrorist action, and the full force of the United States Government would come down on this thing like a hammer. There could be nothing that linked Larry or him to the device. Every component had been outsourced using untraceable broken chains. DNA removed with bleach solution. In truth, he didn't even know Larry's real name.

When they'd first hatched this, Hank had expressed his concern. "Look Larry, if this thing goes off, they're going to look at everyone who had access. The night janitor? Are you kidding? It's like a murder mystery where the butler did it."

He remembered Larry's enigmatic smile. "Hank, when they come looking for Larry Burnham, he's going to be very difficult to find. Larry Burnham doesn't exist."

"What? What do you mean?" Hank had sputtered.

"Hank, we're different people. You're an activist. You've got an office and an internet presence. Your neighbors have known you for years and you've got official fingerprints in the database. The NSA probably has a file on all of your activities."

"And you don't?" Hank was genuinely surprised. "How could you possibly be a modern person here in California and not have a real identity?"

Larry nodded, then said with a smile, "I can't tell you how or I'd have to kill you."

Hank snorted at the joke, but it came up short. Larry had

smiled, but there was something in his eyes that stopped Hank in his tracks. He suddenly didn't want to know any more about Larry.

The crunch of tires on the gravel drive announced an arrival. Hank closed the ice chest lid and crossed the room to the shed door. He pulled it open a crack and saw the generic metallic grey of the generic sedan. Larry, or whoever he was, stood beside the open driver's door, looking about contentedly. With his warm brown skin and dark eyes, shaved head and black beard, he could be any of a hundred men you'd see on the streets of San Francisco any given evening. He was, Hank realized, a generic person. He opened the door fully and waved down. "Hello Larry. Why don't you back it up here."

Larry nodded and slipped back behind the steering wheel. He drove up the dirt road and did a three point turn so that the trunk faced the workshop door. He stepped out and came around to where Hank stood.

"Morning," Larry said, "I really love the smell of the fir trees in the morning." He scanned about appreciatively. "This is such a beautiful place."

"I've got Mr. Lynas ready to go," Hank said and motioned for Larry to follow him inside. "I want to go over a small change on the activator switch. Here, let me show you." Hank lifted the lower right corner of the false bottom. A small gray green box the size of a cigarette packet was nestled at the end. "I put a green LED here. When you turn the knob, green means good to go."

"Neatly done, Hank."

Using his gloves, Hank resettled the Styrofoam corner and laid in the bottles of soft drinks. "You'll need to get the ice and sandwiches when you get back across the bridge. It should all be good if it gets wet, but try to keep the ice in a bag to cut down on the sloshing underneath."

"Got it," Larry replied. "Hi ho silver, away!"

They both grinned, and Hank shut the lid. Larry walked back to the open door and popped the trunk. Hank wedged the ice chest in between a gym bag and a laundry basket filled with shoes, sweatshirts and CDs.

The two men shook hands. They weren't friends. Comrades in arms was a better description.

"I won't say good bye because you were never here," Hank said.

"I never was at all," Larry returned.

He got back behind the wheel and Hank watched the little grey sedan roll down and out of the fenced yard, disappearing around the first corner.

IV
Mendocino, California
1:30 p.m.

The constant whine of the blower was almost, but not quite, background noise. The laughter and cries from the children effectively masked the vaguely industrial growl, and around to the rear of the house, where the patio and pool and bar were located, the cacophony of children at play was reduced to a bearable tinkle.

"Birthday parties for seven year olds are not what they used to be."

Vivien stood at the corner of the house, where she could peek around at the huge inflatable jump house super-slide that had sprouted on the side lawn. Her friend Marjorie nodded in agreement.

"Well, we keep trying don't we? This looks like it will be more of a success than the pony rides we had for Danny's birthday."

Vivien treated herself to a long sip of rosé. "I thought that was a very fun time. Except for Nicola's little boy getting bit."

Marjorie raised her eyebrows and had a pull on her wine. The warm sun made the rosé especially refreshing. "Those Shetland ponies can have a nasty temperament, can't they?" she suggested.

Both women began to giggle. Marjorie held out her glass and Vivien refilled it with cool rosé from the side table.

"Nasty temperament? I suppose so. He shouldn't have been

pulling the pony's tail. If I was the animal, I'd probably have bitten him in the ass too," Vivien smiled archly.

The two women toasted each other and drained their glasses.

A high pitched scream jerked their attention back to the Jump Castle. A little girl was sitting in the middle as two boys jumped up and down on either side of her. When they went down, she went up. Hers was a piercing shriek of delight and the two women drifted back to the pool and bar area. A dozen adults chatted amiably, enjoying small nibbles and the rare sunshine. A little boy covered in what looked like greasy soot ran past, holding a donut.

"You'd think they would have brought out a clean one. I know Bill and Nicola expected better for seven hundred dollars," Marjorie observed.

"My Danny's hands are positively black. He'll need a good scrubbing when we get home. They all will."

"Hi!" Nicola greeted. She walked over to Vivien and Marjorie with a fresh bottle of the rosé.

Nicola was short, with dark curly hair. Her southern Italian roots gave her body strength but not much shapeliness. Both Vivien and Marjorie were a head taller. Vivien a reddish blond, thin, very much an Ashkenazi and proud of her Jewish heritage. Big blue eyes looked huge in her lean face and she accented the fact with tasteful make-up. Marjorie was more of a central European bulldozer, her East Coast upbringing always on display. Her overuse of hairspray and caked make-up were the subject of more than a few catty conversations in their circle of acquaintances, but their children held them together in common cause. For Mendocino, they were the elite. With expensive homes in San Francisco and successful husbands, the three women did have more in common with each other than with most of the regular, full time denizens of the small community.

Nicola poured herself a generous serving of wine, then divided the remainder of the bottle between Vivien and Marjorie. "It's a nice gathering today," Nicola reflected, gazing over the assembly.

The women did make an effort to be a part of the community. As their children made friends locally, they had come to know many of the parents. Mendocino, an artistic coastal outpost in the Northern California wine country, had an eclectic and eccentric element they wanted to cultivate.

"Hello girls! Nice party, Nicole." Helen Bowden strolled over to where the three women stood. Helen was someone Nicola wanted as a friend since she owned one of the better known galleries on the main street.

"Helen, I'm so glad you could be here. Sophie looked so pretty when she came. I'm afraid the Jump Castle will be rather rough on her dress."

Helen shrugged. "Wouldn't be much of a party if the kids didn't get dirty. Is that new piece over the fireplace one of yours? I haven't seen it before."

Nicola smiled delightedly. "It is, thanks for noticing. I brought it up from my studio last month. I keep looking at it though. I'm not sure it's done."

Helen took a sip of her white wine and gazed evenly at Nicola. "Looks done to me. I don't think you'd want to do any more on it."

She looked over Nicola's head, towards the corner of the house, and an expression of exasperation blossomed on her stern features. "Oh Sophie!"

The three friends turned and Marjorie sucked in her breath.

"Oh my god!"

Sophie walked slowly across the deck towards them. Her face and hair were streaked black, as if someone had taken two hands full of axle grease and wiped them down her slim little form from head to toe.

Helen's expression softened at the stricken look on the little girl's face.

"Hey, darling. What have you got yourself into?"

The tenderness in her voice caused the dam to break. Sophie began to sob. "I'm sorry mommy. The big toy got dirty. It's all sticky. My dress..." Her voice trailed off. She held out the soiled folds of her skirt towards Helen and wept disconsolately.

There were a dozen adults gathered around the pool bar. Bill was laughing and pouring wine. He looked over at Nicola and the smile faded from his face. A number of the other adults had stopped talking and were following his gaze. Then a shrieking erupted from around the corner. It wasn't a fun cry, as all the parents recognized instantly. As a group, all the adults moved towards the panicked, childish screaming.

"I don't hear the blower," Vivien blurted out.

The tower with the slide from the top of the Castle was partially collapsed. A little boy, Danny, was stuck to the slide surface. It was draping sideways and he cried and struggled like a fly caught on sticky paper. Another child sat atop the shrinking mass, a tiny bird in a nest filling with black ooze.

A little girl inside the play structure was shrieking in terror, the collapsing sides holding her like a pair of great, black lips. Two other boys stood up to their waists, their feet having penetrated the jumping surface, confused little legless torsos.

Three of the men launched themselves into the melting bounce room and began extricating weeping children, passing them out to the waiting hands of other parents. Marjorie ran to Danny and began tugging at him, desperately trying to extract him from the deepening goo.

"Mommy! Mommy!" he bellowed in terror.

"I'm here, Danny! Mommy's here!"

Oakland, California
Citigen
2:00 p.m.

By mid-afternoon Kyle and Julie had the blueprint for their first Trojan Horse nailed down. Kyle sat back from the keyboard of the sequencer-synthesizer, the GOD machine, and studied the multiple display screens.

Julie entered the lab carrying her laptop before her like a divining rod, reading as she walked.

"How is Whitcombe's team getting along?" Kyle asked.

"I've got their preliminary architecture right here. It looks good, but we're got to run it past GOD and see if it passes muster."

She unplugged the flash drive from the slot on her laptop and inserted it into the sequencer mainframe. It was official policy at Citigen for all computer systems to be de-linked. Information between labs or other departments was hand carried from one isolated system to another, not even a local net was used in-house. The hackers were always probing around the edges, and Citigen's security structure of multiple, isolated pods had so far been successful in thwarting penetration. Personal cellphones and other wireless systems were not allowed on campus.

Kyle gazed for a moment at her flash drive blinking in the slot. "It still amazes me how ingenious the penetration pathways are. Every time somebody gets hit the IT people have their hair blown back, like, wow, didn't expect that one! Remember last year when they hit Mercy Hospital with ransom ware? What would happen if they captured our system somehow and wanted ten million dollars to release our data? Or for that matter, sold all our work to the highest bidder."

Julie was watching the upload bar on the GOD. "I was thinking how similar our Trojan Horse is, like we were imitating the same attack on *Flexilis* that the hackers use on system-linked computer networks."

Kyle smiled at her use of the proposed Latin name for Boogie. *Flexilis comedenti*, the rubber eater. It wasn't official and frankly, he liked Boogie better. Julie had suggested the standard convention of naming a new organism after the discoverer.

"What about *Flexilis comedenti hoffmani*? It's got a nice ring to it," she teased.

Kyle had deferred. "Oh, that would be a nice legacy. Rubber eating little Hoffmans! I think not, Dr. Newsom."

Kyle smiled to himself, remembering the moment. In a way, it had got him thinking more seriously about his relationship with Julie. He wasn't opposed to little Hoffmans running around if that's where the future led with her.

Julie continued her line of thought about the genetic modification techniques. "I mean we've talked about how the macroscopic and the microscopic differ in scale yet similar problems often have similar solutions. We are going into living systems and hacking the DNA. In a very real sense we're hijacking the machinery of life and re-purposing it for our own ends." Julie tapped at a few keys on the board and studied the read-out. Then she swiveled to Kyle. "Don't get me wrong. You know I'm not one of your protestors. There's a world of difference in our intentions here. I'm not making a false equivalency between us and the thieves doing the computer break-ins. Just that the logic needed for breaking into codes and modifying them is similar."

Kyle nodded and grinned. "Gene Hackers we are!"

A small musical tone said the analysis on the Whitcombe proposal was done.

"Here we go," said Kyle, and they read the clearance together. The architecture was stable and unique. It was a go.

"We should be starting the first test run by six o'clock. I'm going to take Dave at his word and initiate the bulk synthesis of both fixes."

Julie nodded. "They said time was of the essence. I'll go down and tell Tom and his group that they hit a homerun. Back in a minute." She collected the flash drive and strolled gracefully out of the room.

They both knew the absurd pressure the lab was under. Not long ago, what had been accomplished in twenty-four hours would have taken years of painstaking work. And now, a daunting list of "ifs" still had to be addressed in the next twelve hours.

If their Trojan Horse would be able to successfully deploy the hack on the DNA target of Boogies carbonase sequence.

If the resultant enzyme mutation was deactivated, unable to break the carbon to carbon bonds.

If the Whitcombe Trojan Horse will slow or halt energy production.

If the propensity for horizontal gene transfer will allow their hacks to transmit to neighboring patches of the fungal mycelium.

Julie re-entered the room grinning broadly. "Tom is taking everybody in their lab out for Italian to celebrate. He and Tina will come back and spell us tonight until the results come in. I'm going up and will get the test series ready, OK?"

"Great, thanks. I'll be up shortly to help."

The tests involved infecting samples of Boogie with the two different hacks and monitoring the results. There wasn't any way to speed that up *in vivo* so it was going to require hands on. There wasn't time to wait for the hack to pass through sexual reproduction. It had to spread like a sneeze in a crowded plane. If this was successful, the fungal organism would need all its versatility to shift metabolic pathways to a more benign, non-plastic eating form.

Programming the synthesizer, Kyle reflected on his afternoon conversation with Dave Davenport. Dave was helping to make the case to the EPA for the emergency waiver. He was a terrific business mind, but his scientific acumen was best at selecting qualified and talented researchers to carry various Citigen projects forward.

"So, explain how this is not like a fungicide," Dave had asked.

"Well, for starters, it isn't an environmental poison. We're sending in two hacks. The first clips out a small bit of the DNA coding in what we believe is a key section of the carbonase enzyme. That's the one responsible for Boogie's ability to break apart molecules of plastics. Our hack should disrupt the way the protein of the enzyme folds, deactivating it."

Kyle knew that Dave understood the 3-D shape of an enzyme was responsible for its activity.

"Why not clip out the entire sequence for the enzyme? Wouldn't that solve the problem?"

Kyle shook his head. "We need to get in under the radar of the DNA repair system. We're only changing twelve base pairs out of more than a thousand coding for the enzyme. If we take it out completely, we'd likely see the migration of a replacement code from surrounding cells. Our scenario suggests that the changes we are making will sufficiently alter the shape of the enzyme, enough to deactivate it *in vivo*. Boogie loses most, if not all of its access to plastic. It's sort of like how the hemoglobin molecule in the red blood cells of people having sickle cell anemia is misfolded. It works, but not like it should."

Dave had nodded, "But it protected against malaria so it persisted in the population."

"Yes, like that," Kyle had agreed.

"The second hack is on the oxidative phosphorylation chain, the pathway that Boogie uses to make ATP after creating the carbon radicals."

Dave blinked on that one so Kyle offered another angle. "You know we breakdown glucose and using oxygen we produce the only form of chemical energy our cells can use - ATP. We give off carbon dioxide and water as waste products along the way. This chain of chemical reactions has a series of steps. If one of the steps becomes blocked, it affects everything downstream. It's like a fountain with water pouring from the highest bowl down to the second highest, then the third highest and so on. If you move bowl number two out of the line, the water cascade stops flowing."

"OK," Dave reflected, "so we've got both the ability of Boogie to melt plastic and its ability to gain energy from that melting dealt with, assuming your designs work. The EPA is going to ask me why we think a broad environmental release of your hacks will not lead to infection in other organisms. My response will be that the DNA sequences are unique and that the Trojan Horse has, as far as we can determine, a one hundred percent specificity. No other living thing on Earth shares those small sections of the DNA profile with the fungus. What else do I need to know?"

Kyle swallowed. They had the same rollout questions with every GMO. They were the right questions to ask. Will the hack affect your target and only your target? The CRISPR-Cfp1 editing complex gave a very high degree of targeting confidence. The sequences the teams had built on did not exist anywhere else in the world genetic data base. But could he say scientifically that it was a hundred percent? Of course not, and that was the rub. It was like being asked to guarantee that a given fingerprint or a snowflake was one hundred percent unique. You can't.

Kyle rubbed the back of his head.

"In this case, we have to make a risk-benefit assessment. If the fungal spores spread unchecked the costs are going to be huge. If next week we find an uncatalogued life form in the Amazon or in a marine trench that shares some of Boogie's profile, there goes the hundred percent certainty."

Dave nodded.

"One last question, Dr. Hoffman. If these hacks are effective, can we be said to be causing the extinction of the organism?" It was more of a PR question than a scientific one.

"Boogie evolved a unique metabolic pathway allowing it to exploit plastic waste as a food supply. If we deny it plastic waste it will likely follow the fungal pattern of creating energy from an alternate metabolic pathway. Members of the species would likely go back to what they were eating before they figured out how to eat plastic. Sort of like how our own cells shift over to fermentation when we run short of oxygen. So I'd venture to say, no, we'll not be causing its extinction. Just pushing it down a different pathway."

At four thirty, Kyle entered the lab with two vials and nodded to Julie. "Well, keep your fingers crossed," he smiled.

They omitted a control tank. Down the road, someone could replicate the work and publish. Right now, peer review was the last thing on the list. Series One would have the carbonase hack,

Series Two the ATP hack and Series Three both. If metabolic activity was reduced or eliminated and the gene transfer allowed the hacks to spread they would have succeeded. The next twelve hours were going to be critical. Kyle had the GOD system going fully into production mode. If the data showed the genetic modification to be successful, they'd have twenty-four hours to do a seeding over the bloom on the gyre. Even a best case scenario would not yield a knock-out blow on Boogie. Too many of the spores had already reached the mainland. But at least they'd have a tool to begin a meaningful mop-up. It would be a little like fighting staph infection in hospital buildings. Even though there are effective sterilization strategies, the spread is pernicious.

"If this works, we'll still be playing whack-a-mole for quite a few years," Kyle reflected, "but the potential of a wide spread infrastructure meltdown will have been greatly reduced."

"Dave is already talking about a patent on the carbonase system," Julie said. "We may have a marketable tool for decomposing plastics and re-purposing the carbon for other projects."

Kyle smiled, "Like making more plastics, huh? Well, it could be worse."

By five thirty the tanks had been inoculated and the waiting game began.

"It looks like we're going to be pulling an all-nighter, Dr. Newsom. How about a dinner break, my treat?" Julie brushed a strand of silky hair behind an ear and grinned at Kyle.

"Well if you're treating, how about the Szechuan Palace?"

"One of my favorites. Let's do a clean-up and meet at the fitness room in, what, half an hour?"

"Oh, twenty is fine for me," she beamed, "It's Saturday night so earlier is better. Especially since we need to get back here to monitor."

VI
Oakland, California
Citigen
8:00 p.m.

"Evening Mike, evening Neal."

Larry nodded to the two gate guards. Mike eyed the ice chest on its folding dolly.

"Hi Larry. Catering dinner?"

Mike smiled mildly but Larry knew the drill.

He laughed, looking down at the chest. "Oh, this? I wish. Spent the day out at Point Reyes Seashore. Didn't make it home to drop off my beach stuff. Here." He settled the ice chest on the ground and casually popped the lid. "Got extra Dr. Peppers and chips."

He pushed the plastic bag with the foot-long Subway sandwich to the side and dug out a bag of Doritos and a couple of drinks, proffering them to the two guards. Neal's eyes lit up. "Great, we're on until midnight." He reached for a drink and the bag of chips. Mike scanned the box contents and seemed satisfied. "Not for me, Larry, thanks. I don't eat after eight. Have a good one. See you on the way out."

Larry nodded and smiled, then inclined his head towards the building. "Quite a few lights on for a Saturday night. What's going on?"

"Oh, they had some mucky-mucks in this morning," Neal offered. "Seems like they've got a big project getting underway. Lot of folks here all day."

Mike looked at Neal with a hint of exasperation. "Yeah, that's so. Less said the better, right." He looked at Neal who got it and nodded. "Thanks for the pop," he said and went inside the security office.

Larry looked at Mike and shrugged. Mike nodded. Neal wasn't the sharpest knife in the drawer.

Inside, Larry made his way to the janitorial service room on the first floor. He changed into his Citigen coveralls, hanging his street clothes neatly in the locker. The fourth floor was his normal starting place and he kept to the routine, taking the lobby elevator up. There were special closets on each floor, with the cleaning supplies and rubbish chutes and bins. The big cleaning was usually on Sunday, when he'd put in eight hours with the vacuum and big floor polisher. Tonight it was just trash collection, the rest rooms and some sweeping. Generally he'd be done before midnight, but he would take a little longer tonight. "Maybe I'm just being paranoid," he thought, but he didn't want to exit while Mike was still on duty, the friendly inquiry of, "Hey, did you forget your ice chest?" That wasn't a conversation he wanted to have tonight.

Starting with the hall sweep, he began to relax. There was no one on this level, administration. Neal's offhand comment had bumped up his anxiety about people in the building, but if there was some big deal going on the administrative offices would not have been empty.

By ten thirty he was beginning the second floor, the production level. Floors three and four were vacant, the corridors illuminated by the low wattage LED lights, but all the offices were put to bed. He wheeled the big canvas rubbish bin down the hall and opened the door to the synthesizer room. The lights were on and the array of machines that constituted the heart of Citigen glowed silently. Or nearly silently. A stainless steel frame housed what always reminded him of a beer bottling assembly. Now and again there was a soft clink of glass as the autofill moved a flask down the line. They were making something alright.

"What sort of new monster tonight?" The thought cracked the door on his fury and the steel in his heart glistened for a moment. "Mr. Lynas has a nice surprise for you."

Now was the time. He retreated to the hall and slipped into the elevator. The ice chest lay undisturbed where he'd parked it against the lockers. "OK, wakey, wakey," he smiled to himself and lifted the corner of the false bottom. With a quick twist he turned the knob on the detonator and Hank's little green light told him all was well with the world. Good idea, that.

Replacing the corner, he actually felt hungry. Larry removed his sandwich and a cool Dr. Pepper. He seated himself at the small service table in the middle of the room. Lunch break. Why not? All nice and normal.

The remote for the wall mounted TV lay on the table, so he flipped on the screen. Because there was no penetration of Citigen by any network, the best he could do was use the table top antenna, duct taped to the top of the TV. It worked for local broadcasts and he pulled in KPIX. The eleven o'clock news was just beginning. Larry bit into his spicy Italian and twisted the top off his Dr. Pepper. The lead story was about the death count in the latest blow up between West Bank residents and Israeli settlers. "They'll have a different lead story tomorrow," he thought, "and I'll be eating Mexican food in Tucson."

Chewing the last bite of his sandwich he vaguely noticed the last story, a piece about customers losing power on the North Coast:

"More than two hundred thousand people from Mendocino to Humboldt are without power tonight after a substation for PG&E collapsed near Eureka, triggering the black out."

"More same old same old" he thought.

Larry flipped off the TV and threw his garbage back into the ice chest. "Why give them any DNA?"

With the lid now closed, he tilted the dolly back and moved into the hall, trailing the cooler. The door to the elevator took a moment to open and when it did he was suddenly confronted by half a dozen faces. It was startling. They stopped talking amongst themselves and gawked at him for a moment, then exited the lift.

"Evening," someone said.

"Evening," Larry replied. They moved down the hall and out toward the car park. He stepped into the elevator with Mr. Lynas and punched the second floor button. A woman in the group, the last to leave, looked back at him curiously over her shoulder. He tapped the Citigen logo on his coveralls and made a "pushing the broom" gesture. She nodded and gave him a hesitant smile. Then she was gone, out the glass doors.

The synthesis room was lit and empty. Larry wheeled Mr. Lynas into the room and parked him against the wall, beside a stack of white cardboard boxes. All quite innocuous.

Back in the hallway, he pulled the canvas bin down towards the restrooms. On the way, he saw light coming out under the door of lab three and heard a pair of voices. Larry looked at his watch. Eleven thirty. What were people doing here at this hour?

He knocked on the door and the talking within stopped. When it opened he recognized the face of Dr. Hoffman, one of the apologists-in-chief for Citigen. He'd seen him on the news trying to provoke a confrontation with protestors in front of the gate a few weeks ago. Now, here he was in the flesh.

The face of a woman, a very attractive woman, appeared from around his shoulder. She seemed surprised.

"Hello. What can I..." and his eyes fell on the trash bin.

"Oh, sorry. We've been working late. You're the night janitor, I take it?"

Larry swallowed and tried to smile. "Yes. Larry Burnham. I'm sorry I disturbed you. I'll just be a moment collecting your baskets," he offered.

Kyle swung the door open. "Yes. Yes, please. Come in. We're just in the middle of some things."

He backed into the room, leaving the door wide open. Larry pushed his bin in and collected the two circular cans at each end of the lab room.

"It's looking good," he overheard.

"Look at the carbon monoxide levels in Series Three," Hoffman said.

"Hmm. Not so good in Series One, though," the woman countered.

Larry cleared his throat to get their attention. "Excuse me. Look, sorry to disturb but I'm wondering about the lights. Will you be here much longer?"

Kyle felt a flash of annoyance with the man. "Don't worry about the lights. We'll be sure to turn them off when we leave." He went back to the readouts on tank three.

"Will that be soon?" Larry asked.

Kyle looked up at the question. The fellow had an odd expression in his eyes. Annoyance rapidly mutated into caution.

"Yes, very soon. Thanks. Don't worry, we'll see the lights are out before we leave."

That seemed to satisfy the man and he departed with an, "Evening."

The door clicked shut.

"Night staff," observed Julie.

"Hmm," Kyle replied.

"Still glad you sent Tom and Tina home?"

"Oh," Kyle replied, "we're here for the duration. They might as well get some sleep. It'll be fine. They'll have a big day tomorrow."

July 22nd

Larry didn't like the fact that at twelve thirty there were still people in the building. They had said they were leaving, but now he stood outside and the lights were still on in the second floor lab. He walked out to the security building and was relieved to see that Mike and Neal were gone. The midnight to eight shift had come on. He knew one of the men slightly.

"Hi Tim," Larry greeted the older man.

Tim looked up from his steaming cup of soup and squinted at him. "Oh, hello Larry. You're here late."

"Not as late as them," he replied, cocking a thumb up towards the second floor.

Tim gazed for a moment towards the second floor. Steam from the cup of soup fogged his glasses. "Hmm. Burning the midnight oil, I guess. They're the last ones."

The right thing to do was call this a miss. He'd go back in, disarm Mr. Lynas and they'd try again another time. It was a shame, after all the planning, but killing people gave the movement a bad name. He'd just have to.

"What the hell is this?" Tim was looking behind Larry, his glasses reflecting flashing blue and red lights. Larry turned to find four squad cars converging on them, now only a few yards away. Where had they come from? His first impulse was to flee, but he checked it immediately and instead held steady, watching the officer approaching him. Men erupted from the other squad cars and fanned out along the perimeter fence. Tim and the other guard gawked at the sudden flurry of activity. Had Mr. Lynas been discovered?

"Evening. Lieutenant Haggerty, Oakland Police."

He showed a small notebook to Larry, Tim and the other guard. The holographic identity card reflected an incongruous rainbow in the overhead LED illumination of the security building.

"What's going on?" Tim asked.

Lieutenant Haggerty sized up the rent-a-cop uniform and Tim's nametag. "We've received a credible threat against this facility, Mr. Robbins."

Larry noticed he didn't call Tim Officer Robbins. Arrogant prick.

At that moment, the policeman turned to Larry. His eyes took in the coveralls and the Citigen logo.

"And you are?"

"Larry Burnham. I'm an employee here, janitorial. I was just getting ready to head for home, but I was concerned about a couple researchers in the building. I can't lock up until they're out."

Lieutenant Haggerty looked up toward the building and back to Larry.

"Can I see some photo ID please?"

He removed what Larry recognized as a portable data scan from his belt and involuntarily his knees felt wobbly. Now rather nonplussed, he pulled out his wallet and offered his driver's license and Citigen photo ID card. The policeman scanned them both with his handheld and passed them back. A tense moment passed until some sort of clearance came through.

"Mr. Burnham, you're off the hook for locking up tonight. I wonder if you'd accompany these officers into the building and locate the researchers you spoke of?"

"Oh, yeah, sure. Let's go."

Three young, clean shaven policemen stood at the ready behind Lieutenant Haggerty.

"Take care," Tim called as they marched up the walk towards the building.

"What sort of credible threat?" Larry asked the officer beside him while they walked.

"There's a group claiming that your lab here is responsible for the Boogie infection hitting the northwest. Saying the disease is your lab created thing. They're threatening to firebomb Citigen in retaliation." The man had a surprisingly high pitched voice and Larry shot him a glance. Very young, early twenties?

Larry almost laughed, he felt such relief. The dark thoughts about Hank turning him in hovering at the edge of consciousness evaporated.

They entered the front doors and an Officer Klein took charge.

"In what room are the researchers, Mr. Burnham?"

Larry nodded to the elevator, "Lab three, second floor."

"Louis, will you conduct Mr. Burnham to his belongings and see him off the premises. Colin, you're with me."

"Let's collect your gear Mr. Burnham. I'll see you back down to the security gate." It was the young man with the high voice.

Within ten minutes, Larry found himself in his street clothes back at the entry. There were now half a dozen squad cars scattered around the parking area, lights flashing. He checked his watch. In an hour and a half, Mr. Lynas was going to blow. He knew with sickening certainty there would be casualties if he didn't make the call.

"Jesus Christ, if I use my cell they'll be all over me before I can get going. Need to find a payphone," he reflected.

There was time. Tell them there was a bomb in the building and they had to pull everybody back. This could still work and the firebomb threat group would draw off the dogs! He started his car and drove slowly away from the flashing lights.

"Payphone. Where do you find a payphone. A bar...no!" He had it. Coming out of Yoshi's Jazz Club a few weeks back, behind the parking structure. At the time he'd joked to Karen, "Hey. Look at that. Superman still has a few changing rooms in town."

The phone was five minutes away and on his way home. This would work. He accelerated. By one-forty he was headed down Washington toward Jack London Square. The streets were bleak, deserted.

The little booth was illuminated. Larry left his car idling as he slipped inside. The 911 emergency was toll free but he'd be immediately located by the dispatcher. If there was a squad car in the neighborhood he'd be nailed.

Conveniently, the Oakland Fire Department was listed on the old black phone box. He'd tell whoever answered about the bomb and not wait around for questions. They'd get the message. He'd hightail it to Berkeley and follow the exit plan.

Fifty cents. Larry fumbled around in his pocket and came up with a quarter, a nickel and three pennies. Shit. OK, parking meter change bottle in the glove box. He exited the booth and walked the five feet back to his passenger door, reached into the glove box and extracted the change bottle.

Before he could straighten up and close the door, a voice said, "Hey man. You got any spare change?"

The voice had come from behind him and he turned to face four men forming a small semi-circle around him. Their young faces were illuminated by the interior car lights. Larry looked left and right. His heart sank at the isolation.

"Hey guys. This is an emergency. Give it a miss this time, OK?"

"Oh, an emergency. You got an emergency?"

A white kid with a pock marked face and mean little eyes glared at him. His compatriots, a black kid and a couple of Latino gang bangers, smiled mirthlessly.

"We got an emergency too, *pachuco.*"

One of the Latinos held a knife forward, hard menace in his eyes. The others looked like they might be holding something too, but out of sight.

Larry thought about diving back into the car through the open passenger door and hitting the accelerator with his hand, get fifty feet down the road and take off. But the white kid was fast. The blow he aimed at Larry's face glanced off at his quick dodge, but a rain of fists knocked him to his knees and he sprawled out onto the sidewalk. Hands tugged at his pockets.

"Got it. Get the ATM."

A hard kick to his face and the taste of blood in his mouth. Then his head was jerked up by a hand gripping his beard. Another hand held his ATM card in front of him.

"Code, motherfucker. The right one. The first time," sneered Pock Marks.

He was beat. Let them have it. "Forty nine forty nine," he managed through his mangled lips.

"Oh, a Niners fan. The Raiders kill the Niners."

Larry felt the knife point enter his throat and jerk sideways. The warm rush down his shirt was strangely painless.

II
Oakland, California
Citigen
1:23 a.m.

Kyle stood facing the smooth face of Officer Klein.

"I don't care. We don't have time for more conversation. We cannot depart the building. Speak to your supervisor again and explain. This," he waved an arm towards the tanks, "is in a critical stage. Better, tell your supervisor to call the Department of Homeland Security. Go right to the top and do it now. This process cannot be interrupted."

Julie was wide-eyed, watching the exchange from the computer desk. The other young officer was strangely nonchalant, looking around the lab as if searching for something. He felt her eyes on him and met her gaze, smiling. He bowed slightly. "Evening, ma'am. Sorry to disturb you. But better safe than sorry."

Both Kyle and Julie were taken aback when the firebomb threat was revealed. Kyle, usually not quick to anger, had flared, "Stupid bastards. We're the ones trying to save their sorry asses."

Julie was a bit surprised at his French, but felt pretty much the same. It was late, they were under a lot of pressure and exhausted. They didn't need this crap added to the pile. Up until the point when the two officers had entered the lab, indicators had been good. Very good, really. All three series were showing marked decreases in metabolic activity. In one more hour they would gene sequence samples from each run to determine if the hacks had been successfully transmitted.

At Kyle's insistence the two police removed themselves to the hallway and spoke over their radios to command.

"Yes sir, that's what he said, directly to DHS. Yes sir. That's right. OK, we'll sweep this building."

Officer Klein clicked off his collar mike and looked at Colin. "We'll start on the fourth floor and sweep back down to here. We may have to hog-tie the good doctors to get them out of here."

Colin's eyes widened but he shrugged and replied, "Let's go."

III
Oakland, California
Citigen
2:19 a.m.

"Kyle, look at this!"

Julie must have been as exhausted as he was but somehow she managed to appear fresh and awake. "Series Three has bottomed out. No discernable metabolic activity. Series One is down ninety-three percent and Series Two by eighty-seven percent. I think we've done it."

Her eyes glistened with excitement. She stood and moved to where Kyle was peering into one of the bubbling tanks and placed her delicate hand over his. He tore his attention away from the water and gazed at her. The dark circles under his eyes were new. "Yes, Dr. Newsom, I think we have."

He embraced her and kissed in a way they had never done before, warriors and lovers.

Of course there was a knock on the door. Officer Klein stood outside, looking grim. "You've been cleared to stay in the building but we need to place a team with you for your own safety." He entered, followed by another pair of young, uniformed officers.

"This is Officer Swan and Officer Hodges. If you need anything, they'll call out for you."

Kyle nodded to Swan, an attractive Asian woman with a no-nonsense expression. Hodges looked to be Latino, youngish, dark mustache.

"We'll be needing to bring test samples to the synthesizer lab shortly. That's two doors down on the right," Kyle announced. "Thank you for your help, Officer Klein. It's late and we're in the final stages of work. Interruption was not an option."

"They explained to me, Dr. Hoffman. Good luck."

He nodded to the security team and strode off down the hall.

Julie had been setting up the sample series for genomic analysis and now they moved to the sequencer-synthesizer. Flashing red and blue lights from the parking lot below bounced around the hallway. Kyle thought it looked incongruously festive, a techno-dance party.

There were few non-technical places to sit in the lab and after about fifteen minutes Swan and Hodges removed themselves to a position just outside the door. The padded bench in the hall offered a more comfortable waiting spot. Kyle began the sample sequencing. If the hacks had been passed on their codes would show up in the non-inoculated mycelium all down the line. The probability was very high that they had succeeded, given the lab results, but this critical confirmation step needed to occur before they could deploy. If the hacks hadn't spread like a common cold it was back to the drawing table.

He glanced over to the synthesizer output. More than a hundred liters of each hack had already been produced. By morning, it would be double that. Figure a per bottle cost of maybe ten thousand dollars. If it was useless, that would be a lot of money on its way to the incinerator. On the other hand, if it was effective, they be able to do an aerosol dispersal over a very large part of the bloom before the winds swept the spores inland.

"Were you ever a night owl?" Julie asked.

Kyle grinned, "Oh, in College there were more than a few

times I'd be up this late cramming for exams. And of course, wild parties on the beach."

"I'd like to have known you in those days," she laughed. "Do you think we'd have gotten along?"

"Gotten along?" Kyle mused, "I think I would have been afraid to talk to you."

The stress and the exhaustion were taking a toll. Julie sank down on the bench beside him and leaned against his shoulder. "I was nobody to be afraid of. A mousy pre-med student with her nose in a book. I hid in my books."

He reached around and across her back, gently pulling her into him. They leaned into each other.

A whirring click startled them both. Had they fallen asleep? It was nearly three in the morning.

Julie stretched. "It's been awhile since I napped sitting up. How are we doing?"

Kyle was at the monitor desk, studying the sequencer results on his screen, nodding. "We are doing…great!"

She came close and leaned over behind him, her trim body draped over his back. They studied each read-out as it scrolled across the monitor. Kyle covered her hand with his, then turned to face her.

"Dr. Newsom, I think we have just saved the world," he grinned.

"My hero!"

They held each other in a sweet and lingering kiss.

Three a.m.

IV
Oakland, California
Citigen
3:00 a.m.

The concussion knocked Lieutenant Haggerty off his feet, propelling him backwards through the air into the parking lot. It was like being hit by a solid wave from head to toe. He was picked up and carried, the impact knocking the wind out of him. His mind registered the expanding orange black ball of fire that had replaced the space of the building. Only his military training saved him. He automatically rolled for cover under the SUV he had slammed into. The shrapnel of the building cut apart anyone left lying in line of sight.

A few pieces continued to rain out of the sky. Tim staggered out of the security building and gaped at the sudden desolation around him. The shattered bodies of some of the young policemen lay scattered on the ground, silent and unmoving. A strange tinkling reverberated in the air in the aftermath of the blast. It reminded him of the sound his little glass wind chimes made in a gentle breeze.

"Lordy! Oh, Lordy," he murmured to nobody in particular

V
Lagunitas, West Marin, California
8:20 am

"What would life in the country be without roosters crowing," Joan thought. She rolled over in the big king bed and pulled a pillow over her head. "Quiet. Quiet on a Sunday morning. Wouldn't that be original."

But it was no use. She was awake enough now to know she needed to use the toilet. With a sigh, she lifted off the pillow. Hank's side was empty. There was a vague remembrance of him getting out of bed and flushing, the slight click of the bedroom door shutting. This time of year it was full light by five twenty in the morning and he was an early riser. She would have preferred snuggling into his back and returning to dreamland, but dropping off alone, in the quiet of the morning, worked too. Except for that rooster.

She slipped into her red kimono and padded out toward the kitchen barefoot. The aroma of fresh coffee in the cool air of the morning was delicious. There was Hank sitting in the breakfast nook, intent on the screen of his laptop. Normally he'd greet her and offer to make her favorite hot mocha. Not this morning it seemed.

"Morning. How'd you sleep," she asked, almost on autopilot, approaching the French Press. Hank looked up with an odd sort of smile on his face. "Good morning. Sorry, I'm remiss." He eased out of the corner and was behind her at the counter in three steps. His large arms closed around her and he nuzzled at her hair. "Let me make you my famous Mocha Java."

Joan felt the shiver of pleasure she always had when he held her like this. "That would be most appreciated, sir. I've always depended on the kindness of strangers." She twisted around and hugged him back.

The breakfast table had the Sunday Chronicle spread around near where Hank was sitting. As usual, he had the comics section in front of him. Not as usual was the glowing screen of his laptop, covering the comics.

Hank reached up into the cupboard and brought down her special mug. It was from one of their first road trips together, a lovely porcelain with a good handle and thin lip. "The Benbow Inn" was emblazoned in green, arching over a motif of redwoods.

She stood beside him now at the counter, watching with amusement as he fumbled the cocoa powder. The short trip from the can to the cup with a heaping tablespoon was fraught with risk.

"Whoops! Come on you, in the cup," he mumbled.

She'd wipe off the counter later as she always did after one of his creations. He added a generous portion of whole milk and an extra spoon of sugar. After a quick stir he slipped the entire mug into the microwave and hit the "extra minute" button.

"One Meyer's Mocha Java on its way."

Joan smiled and made her sleepy way over to the breakfast table. She poked around at the paper and found the Insight section. The Chronicle was OK as a paper, but for real news she depended on the local progressive radio KPFA and the web site of The Nation.

"Anything interesting in the world this morning?" she asked.

The microwave beeped and Hank lifted out the steaming mug and filled it the rest of the way with strong coffee. With a final flair and only a small spill he stirred the mix and delivered it to the table.

"Well you won't find it in The Chronicle because it happened early this morning." He nodded to his open laptop. "It seems that some group called Gaia Fist blew up your friends at Citigen last night."

Joan, in the middle of taking a sip, put the mug back down on the table. "Blew up my friends? What are you talking about?"

Hank swiveled the laptop so she could read the screen and scrolled back to the headline.

"This," he said.

Terrorist Attack In Oakland

"Oh my God!" she gasped. She pulled the laptop closer and read: "Oakland was rocked early this morning by a huge explosion at local bioengineering firm Citigen. Witnesses said the explosion shattered windows in a six block area. The Citigen facility was completely destroyed by the blast, with early reports describing numerous fatalities. A heretofore unknown eco-terrorist group calling itself Gaia Fist has claimed responsibility.

"In a statement Oakland Police Chief Darryl Green said a number of officers were dispatched to the Citigen campus shortly after receiving the telephoned warning in the early hours of Sunday morning. He said the caller threatened an imminent firebombing of the facility in retaliation for Citigen's accidental release of a powerful bio-agent now causing disruptions in the Pacific Northwest."

Joan stopped reading.

"Who is Gaia Fist?"

Hank tilted his head to the side and seemed almost wry when

he answered, "Gaia Fist is a group that is now in very deep shit."

Joan turned back to the screen and continued the story, sipping her mocha intently. Hank pulled the Insight section over and began reading an article about City Hall's latest effort to deal with homelessness in the South of Market area. He snorted at a paragraph about a new wall paint that caused urine to splash back on the feet of the urinator.

"This is terrible Hank. There were people in the building, police and some of the research people they think. This Gaia group has crossed the line."

Hank shifted and shrugged. "Well I don't suppose they were trying to kill anybody. I mean who would expect the building to be full of people at three a.m. on a Sunday?"

Joan considered.

"This says that the threat to bomb the place was made in the early hours of Sunday morning, so after midnight some time. What did they think was going to happen after doing that? No, this was deliberate. They wanted people in there when the bomb went off. This is murder."

Hank didn't know who "they" were but he felt almost elated that the trail now led away from him and Larry. He wondered where Larry was right now. Then he had a dark suspicion. "What if Larry made the call to get people in there?"

It disquieted him to think that maybe he had helped a murderer to kill people. Nobody was supposed to get hurt on this. Larry, or whoever he was, better disappear.

After their Sunday brunch of avocado omelettes Hank was feeling increasingly uncomfortable. He didn't mean for anyone to die. It wasn't meant to go like this. A deep yearning blossomed in him, the need to go out into nature and cleanse himself.

"Hey darlin', how about putting together a picnic and paddling the big kayak over to Marshall Beach for lunch? It looks clear on Tomales Bay today."

Joan smiled at him tenderly. She could feel Hank's troubled spirit and knew he needed that connection with the natural world just now. It always renewed him. Some words on love from Kahlil Gibran's *Prophet* floated up into her consciousness. About how the pillars of the temple don't stand too close together.

"Why don't you go on your own this time? I think I'd like to go into town and hear the service at church this morning. I'll stop and get baby back ribs with corn on the cob for tonight."

Hank grinned and felt lighter. It was a part of their relationship he loved, the listening to each other's heart. Baby back ribs were just about the last thing an aspiring vegetarian would cook, but she knew he adored them. She was quite a woman.

His old pick-up truck wasn't much to look at, but it started right up and ran well. Hank backed up to the side of the carport where his kayaks were stored. The two single person poly kayaks rested in their cradles above his masterpiece. He had built the long, sleek wooden two person boat himself and it was his pride and joy. Today however, just going out alone for a paddle, one of the polyethylene craft would be adequate. They were a lot easier to toss in the truck and manage by himself.

"God, look at this thing!"

The yellow polyethylene was coated with the crusty black mold that constantly rained down from the Bay Laurels on this side of the hill.

"I love the Bays but they do make a mess of things," he thought.

The kayak was dirtier than it should have been, being tucked in under the eaves of the carport. Hank grabbed a double ended paddle from the rack and tossed it into the bed of the truck. When he grabbed the kayak to lift it out of the cradle, the greasy wetness of the surface surprised him. He stopped. His hands were coated with a black, oily film. Inside the kayak was a pool that looked like someone had poured their oil change waste into his boat. Vandalism? A flash of anger zinged up from the lower brain. Who the hell would do this? He'd been harassed before because of his work with WRAP, but those were mostly ugly phone calls or angry notes. Some local people resented the change he represented.

He lifted the kayak out of the cradle and settled it on the ground.

"Just have to mop it out and wash it here. Can't take this mess out into Tomales Bay," he thought.

He walked into the shed where Mr. Lynas no longer resided. The anger he felt toward the vandals modulated into a grim satisfaction. "We got you, you bastards. Your zombies can take their GMOs and shove them."

He pulled a big, black plastic yard waste bag off the roll and grabbed a handful of old shop towels.

"Have to sop up the oil and take it to recycle next week."

From the corner of the shop, he also snagged the bucket of car wash supplies and moved back up the hill to the car port.

Hank made a pass with the rag and it drank up the oil. He made a second pass, pushing down hard into the bottom of the boat. With a suddenness that startled him, the wad of rag and his hand went right through the hull. He jerked back. The oil began to run out of the new, gaping hole onto the ground.

"What the hell?" he thought.

VI
West Coast of the Olympic Peninsula, Washington
Ocean Shores
4:15 pm

"Fred! Fred, come look. It's a Black Bellied Plover, I'm sure."

Kaly, on the front porch, swiveled her stool around and scanned the living room. Fred wasn't there.

"Where did he go now?" she said to herself.

Out across East Ocean Shores Boulevard, the waters of Grays Harbor glistened in the afternoon light. They'd chosen this house for their retirement because of the view and the proximity to the Oyhut Wildlife Recreation Area. Birding had become a passion for them both.

Kaly had a sip of her beer and returned to the big binoculars. The Vortex 10 x 50 were great birding glasses so long as she had the tripod. They were too heavy and unwieldy for walking excursions, but sitting here on the front porch they were perfect.

She slowly scanned along the breakwater until she spotted a Black Oystercatcher on the prowl. Its round yellow eyes and powerful orange beak were a brilliant contrast to its glossy, black plumage. The mussels had no defense for the lightning strikes of that hard beak.

A clunk behind her pulled her attention back to the living room. There he was!

"Fred," she called, her smokey, whisky voice something he never tired of hearing.

"What is it Kaly? Got somebody good in view?"

She laughed. They were both in their late seventies, but the playfulness of their early days had carried through the years. With her short, blond curls and lively, intelligent eyes, diminutive Kaly was the soul of beautiful pixie. Fred, not much taller and thin as a rice stalk, positively glowed when he gazed at her. After all these years she was still his darling.

"Somebody good? Oh my God Fred, where were you earlier? We had a Black Bellied Plover right in front here."

"That would be the first one this season, wouldn't it?" Fred asked.

"It would," Kaly cheerfully agreed.

"What were you doing?"

Fred bent down and lifted the new portrait for her to examine.

"Finishing," he replied.

Kaly picked up her polyurethane beer cozy and had a sip of the cool brew. She stood and moved into the living room to inspect the painting.

"That's good Fred. You did a better job on the mouth. I think Kurt would approve," she grinned.

Inland, across Grays Harbor was their main shopping town of Aberdeen. It wasn't a big place, but it had the distinction of being the hometown of Kurt Cobain, one of the founders of Nirvana. The Kurt Cobain Memorial Park drew a steady stream of Nirvana fans and others, curious to see the memorial. Fred supplemented their Social Security income with sales of his Kurt Cobain portraits. On a good weekend he'd bring in three or four hundred dollars. Not a fortune, but it helped keep the wolves from the door, he'd joke.

Fred looked down at the finished portrait.

"Is the hair OK?"

Kaly moved around beside him. She slipped her thin arm around his waist and gave a little hug.

"The hair is fine. You always do the hair well, Fred. I don't know why you fret so."

"The Jimi Hendrix still hasn't sold," he said gloomily.

"Well maybe the people coming to the Kurt Cobain Memorial don't care about Jimi Hendrix, Fred."

"Both Bob Marleys sold in one day," he answered, a bit defensive.

Kaly sighed.

"Well there's no accounting for taste, is there. Come here. I want you to see the Oystercatcher if he's still there."

She tugged lightly on his sleeve and returned to her stool on the porch. She had another sip of beer as she settled herself.

"Oh what's this!" she complained, holding out the beer cozy. It was wet and greasy, the Red Eagle decal coming off on her hand.

Fred came up and looked at the mess. He reached for the painting rag that still draped from his rear pocket. "Here. Wipe off with this. Looks like the mosquito repellent strikes again," he smiled.

Kaly looked perplexed. "I didn't use any mosquito repellent, Fred. Oh, never mind. Here, look at this."

She finished wiping off her hand and passed the rag back to Fred. Turning to the binoculars, she scanned along the breakwater.

"Phooey! He's not there now. Oh, look at this, coming in under full sail." She tilted the binoculars up a notch and twiddled the focus. "Nice boat. They're coming in fast."

Fred pulled up a stool beside her and leaned over toward the glasses.

"Coming straight in. Wonder who it is? I don't recognize the boat."

Kaly strolled into the kitchen and pulled a new polyurethane beer cozy out of the drawer. She loaded it with a new can of Corona. When she got back to the front porch Fred was still watching the boat. It was quite close now, less than half a mile from the harbor entry.

"He's going to need to trim some sail," Fred said.

A pod of five kayaks had come around from North Jetty and were making their way into Grays Harbor. The sailboat careened towards them.

"What's he doing, Fred? Can't he see those people in the kayaks?" Kaly's voice had taken on an anxious edge. She stood against the railing looking out.

"Jesus Christ," blurted Fred, "What's the matter with that asshole?"

They watched helplessly as the sailboat tore through the line of kayaks. The paddlers had seen it coming, but knowing they had right-of-way had continued on. Only at the very last moment had they realized the boat was neither turning nor reefing sails. Some fancy back-paddling got them out of harm's way. Fred and Kaly could plainly hear the shouted curses from the kayakers.

"Holy shit!" Fred shouted as the sailboat tore into the rocks of the jetty, a terrible ripping and tearing echoing through the hull. The wind kept pushing the sail and the stern swung around facing them, the bow already beginning to sink. The whole boat heeled over against the rocks, the sail ripping free.

"Well, that's it for *Dickies Treat*," Fred said flatly.

A mob of seabirds swirled around the stern deck of the wallowing ship, diving into the cockpit. Fred looked through the binoculars and gasped at the vivid, wet red beaks of the departing birds.

"What are they eating?" he asked.

About the Author

Vernon St. Clair Castle is a third generation Californian, born in 1951. He grew up in Los Angeles, California and attended UCLA as a pre-med student and graduated with a BS in Zoology and minor in Biochemistry.

His family were ranchers in the northern reaches of Los Angeles County but after the death of his father in 1952, his mother moved to the city where she worked as a designer.

After nearly a decade of travel and work around the world he married in 1984 and undertook the life of family and householder. The decade of travel included a formative period in Asia during the early 1980's when he explored the reality of becoming a Theravada Buddhist monk.

For the last thirty five years Vern has lived and worked in West Marin, California. He taught the sciences in both public and private schools until his retirement in 2013.

Currently he and his wife Renee, an encaustic and watercolor artist, divide their new "rewired" lives between Indonesia, Mexico and West Marin, California.

For more information, including a photo gallery, or to contact the author please go to www.vernoncastle.com